LYON HUNTS AND HUMOR

LYON HUNTS AND HUMOR

True Life Hunting and Adventure Stories

by
Tolbert James "Shorty" Lyon

Sunstone Press
Santa Fe, New Mexico

"Department Profile: T.J. "Shorty" Lyon reprinted by permission of NEW MEXICO WILDLIFE Magazine, New Mexico Department of Game and Fish. "Predator Control Pays High Dividends on Diamond Bar Ranch" and "Bears" reprinted by permission of NEW MEXICO STOCKMAN Magazine.
"Shooting In The Dark," "Lion In The Street," "Very Big Lion," "Lion In My Lap," "No Defense," "A Month of Lions," "Lion Wasn My Aim," and "A Spoiled Lion" reprinted by permission of OUTDOOR LIFE Magazine.

First Edition

Library of Congress Cataloging in Publication Data:

Lyon, Tolbert James, 1907-
     Lyon hunts and humor : true life hunting-adventure stories / by Tolbert James "Shorty" Lyon. – 1st ed.
          p.   cm.
     ISBN: 0-86534-148-6   : $12.95
     1. Hunting–New Mexico.   2. Zoology–New Mexico.   3. Adventure and adventurers–New Mexico.   4. Lyon, Tolbert James, 1907-
I. Title.
SK109.L96   1990
799.29789–dc20   90-37549
                                                                              CIP

Published in 1990 by SUNSTONE PRESS
                    Post Office Box 2321
                    Santa Fe, NM 87504-2321 / USA

DEDICATIONS: to my wife, Louise, who put up with me and my hounds, kept the three mile pipe line running, knew every cow on the range, and would carry on when I was late, or gone for weeks at a time.

● to my daughter, Jennie, who owns a big interest in me and my kingdom, encouraged my creative efforts, and made coming home to supper an event.

● to my son, Jimmy, who caused me no trouble, who ranches and hunts with his sons and married a wife of gold.

● to my friend and boss, Mr. Elliott S. Barker, who swapped stories with me around the camp-fire, and last but not least, blazed the trail to the publishers for me.

● to my friends, young and old all over this wide domain of mine, who gave me and my dogs company and comfort, no matter the time of day or night.

Jennie
Lyon Feather

5

CONTENTS

LIST OF ILLUSTRATIONS

Illustration for:

Drawings on pages 5, 17 and 73 by Virginia L. Feather.

Photographs of Author on pages 2, 6, 116 and 119.

PREFACE

Tolbert James "Shorty" Lyon was a self-made naturalist, a frontiersman, a pioneer in modern times. Born in 1907 no matter what the job he always found himself huntin-trapping and ready to tell a good story.

As a child he often kept meat on the table and a few cents in the sugar bowl with his skills in hunting squirrels, rabbits and possum along the Canadian river in Oklahoma.

As a young man he freighted to Alaska, worked among the Frenchmen loggers in Canada, sang the working songs with Black crews along the leevies in Oklahoma and worked with the toughest of men in the oil fields.

As a young man of twenty-four years with wife and babies he homesteaded in New Mexico in 1931 and at last found his country . . . with the children in school he worked in the gold and silver mines of Mogollon. There he learned "duele mi cabeza" then moved to top ground to the mills. Soon after he started his own wood business where he could make a living and be outdoors. The woodyard was a family affair working hard all summer to gain a week off camping out and fishing in their favorite meadow at Willow Creek. A woodcutter, but also a father, he routinely found himself stopping a heavily loaded truck on the way down the mountain for a small velvet flower spied by a little girl on the way up to the mesa that morning.

Working for the State Department of Game and Fish he was paid for what he was bound to do anyway. He was a conservationist long before the word became popular. He had a great respect for animal life, and that included man, often helping them out in the wilderness and annually giving them a hand out of Silver Creek canyon in deep snow. When extra late coming home he was usually spending long, cold hours to keep an animal from suffering unnecessarily.

When the mining camp closed down in 1942 he became a rancher which suited his wife and son while the daughter was off to New Mexico State University. The population left Mogollon overnight so he became a man of property.

From his stories one can see a man who was extremely happy in the thick of a good hunt, hearing the baying of the hounds. He was never lost, even in a city.

His poems show a zest for life and a good sense of humor, as with *Frost Is On the Windshield* and *The Pick-up Cowboy.*

After thirty-five years with the state department, retiring in 1972 he went to Mexico to hunt the "tigre" and to Venezuela as a guide, then welcomed the quiet life as a wheat farmer on the Arizona, New Mexico border. The last adventure was on the Hopi reservation in Arizona where he was hired to teach their young people the art of trapping. There the Indians made him a "blood-brother" of which he is very proud. He wrote about the Hopi Corn story which they are going to use in their school books.

In November of 1986 he was inducted into the New Mexico Trappers Hall of Fame, an honor shared with three other New Mexico hunters at the time along with the famous "Kit" Carson — now on display at the Kit Carson House Museum in Taos.

He was a self-educated man who found school at the eighth grade a luxury, but never forgot his favorite teachers' names. He treasured good books and friendships and admired the truly educated person. Born in Mena, the fifth child after four sisters, while crossing the Arkansas-Oklahoma border from Missouri, a young brother was born later. His father spoke Dutch, his mother was English-Irish. He claimed to be Mark Twain's fifth cousin. His talents and humor bear this out, but no one sought proof.

Jennie

Virginia L. Feather
1990

Profile of T.J. "Shorty" Lyon
from the *New Mexico Wildlife*

To best know Shorty Lyon, one needs to know something of the town where he has lived the last 35 years and of the country surrounding that town. The man, the town and the country are equally intriguing.

For about 30 miles, U.S. 180 runs north and south through western New Mexico. Its path is almost parallel to the New Mexico-Arizona state line, about 15 miles on the New Mexico side. About three miles north of the small village of Glenwood, the highway traverses an arroyo-cut bench that breaks off into rugged canyons to the west and rises to towering mountains to the east. There, a narrow paved road, N.M. 78, turns east.

A traveler turning there and stopping to read the large historical marker sign would learn that the mountains he was facing were the Mogollons. He would learn that they and the town of Mogollon (Muggy-ON) about eight miles distant over a narrow twisting mountain road, were named after Don Ignacio Flores Mogollon, Governor of New Mexico, 1712-1715. He would learn that, as early as 1912, Mogollon was a thriving mining town with mines having such names as The Last Chance, Maud's, The Deep Down, Silver Queen, The Peacock and Little Fanney.

It would take very little imagination on the traveler's part to know that he was only a short distance from a peek into a portion of the American Southwest's colorful past.

Much of Mogollon's past was already history when Shorty

Lyon arrived there with his family in 1936. Since that time, Shorty has played his part in the history of that area and has even brought national attention to Mogollon, now a ghost town, through his articles which have appeared in the pages of *Outdoor Life*.

T.J. (Shorty) Lyon came to New Mexico from Oklahoma in 1931 and homesteaded at Quemado. Trapping coyotes and selling the pelts was his major source of income.

It was six or seven years later that he moved to Mogollon — Shorty says 1936 and Mrs. Lyon says 1937 — but they both remember it was a cold winter day. The main street of Mogollon had a thick covering of ice, sprinkled with sawdust in an effort to keep it from being so slippery.

"I had my wife and two little kids with me in an old Chevy truck," Shorty remembers. "The population of Mogollon was about 2,000 at the time. The mines had attracted some pretty rough people and there were a lot of them on the street when we got here."

Shorty parked the truck on the main street and went to inquire about finding work. A little while later, he returned. "Well, what do you think of it?" he asked his wife.

"I'll tell you one thing." she answered, "I won't stay here long."

That was 35 — or 34 — years ago.

For 25 of those years, Shorty has been employed by the Department of Game and Fish as a trapper and a lion hunter. From a New Mexico-Arizona part of the country that has produced a number of famous lion hunters, Shorty's name will be remembered among the best of them.

But he is more than a trapper and hunter; he's a writer, a home-spun philosopher and a story teller. If there's anything Shorty does better than hunting lions and trapping predators, it's telling a story. He can keep a listener on the edge of his seat hour upon hour with tales of the early days in Mogollon or of lions, hounds, mules and mountain country.

Shorty is more of a story teller than a writer. "I never got much education," he says. "I didn't finish the seventh grade and I was a poor scholar, never learned much English — spelling, abbreviations, that sort of thing — but even then, when the teacher said write a composition, I could really tell a story."

Shorty's articles have been his stories, just as he tells them, only he has put them down on paper. *Outdoors Life* has bought several of these stories — six or seven Shorty says — and his lion hunting adventures have thrilled readers all over the country.

Some of the titles have been *Lion in the Street, Lion in My Lap, A Month of Lions,* and *Very Big Lion.* His latest, *A Spoiled Lion,* appeared in the Feb., 1970, issue.

Asked to repeat one of the stories briefy, Shorty referred to *Lion in the Street* as one of the best.

"This beat up, old lion came in out of Mexico and walked right down the main street of Mogollon," Shorty says. "The Postmaster had a little dog and this lion jumped on the dog right in front of the Post Office. The Postmaster was an old fellow and couldn't see too good. He looked out and thought it was big dog fighting his little dog and he ran out and gave that lion a good kick. It turned around and snarled and the old fellow saw it was a lion and ran back in the Post Office."

Shorty came along soon after that and had one of his dogs with him. The Postmaster ran out and told him that a lion had killed his dog right in the street. "I couldn't believe it at first," Shorty said. "But then I saw the blood and the tracks. I turned my dog loose and he ran that lion on top of the store. They fought up there, but I couldn't get a shot. Finally, the lion went on down below town in some bluffs and the dog followed him and treed him and I killed the lion there."

As with most good story tellers, that story reminded Shorty of another one, actually a story within a story. Shorty had a mule that he rode during a lot of his hunting adventures. He named the mule Lupie and became quite fond of her.

"Lupie was pretty ornery when I first got her and she was just a young mule," Shorty remembered. "I had a camp over in the Springtime Canyon Country and she got away from me the first night. I wasn't too worried because I was camped near the only water in the country and I knew she would have to come back to water and I could catch her.

"But Lupie was pretty smart and she came back to water when I was out running my trap line. I found tracks where she had been coming to water. Well, finally I built a corral around the water hole and put a gate on it; then I brushed out all the old tracks so I could be sure she was going in. Sure enough, when I came in from running the traps, I found where she had been to water.

"So, the next day I hid under a juniper and waited for her. While I was waiting. I got to thinking about these two lions I had killed some months before in some bluffs down on the Arizona border and thinking that it would make a good story. I went back to camp, got a pencil and pad and wrote most of the story while I was hiding waiting for that mule. Finally, when I was about through with the story she came in, stopped at the gate and looked and sniffed around and then went on in and started drinking.

"I had planned to just slip up and close the gate and I don't know why, but I got to wondering what she would do if I yelled at her and rushed the gate. I knew I could beat her to the gate, so I let out a squall like an Indian and tore out from under that juniper to the gate. It couldn't have worked better. Old Lupie almost jumped out of her skin and was so surprised she didn't even make a run for the gate."

Shorty likes to tell of his early days in Mogollon. He and his family were there nine days before he got a job. Then he went to work in the mine on the grave yard shift making 28 cents an hour. It was hard work under tough conditions. Shorty tells of coming out of the mine shaft once and the foreman asking how much work they had done. "We broke the record," Shorty told him, referring to the amount of ore that had been mined. The foreman's only comment was, "Oh! What else did you break?"

The gold and silver deposits of the mines were never cleaned out, but the mines had to close during the war because it was impossible to get supplies and equipment. They never were reopened because, after the war, rising costs had made it impossible to work them at a profit.

Now Mogollon is a ghost town; its only industry is attracting tourists to an art gallery, museum and the once busy mining buildings that are now falling into shambles.

Of the 2,000 or more people that inhabited Mogollon when Shorty and his family moved there, only he and his wife are left. They moved into the mine superintendent's house in 1946 when Shorty went to work for the Game Department and have lived there since as overseers of property still owned by Lehigh Metals Co., of Pennsylvania. A few other people have moved in over the years and, including Shorty and his wife, Mogollon now has eight year-around residents.

Shorty says, "I've had about the grandest job in the world for the last 25 years. I have been doing what I want to do and getting paid for it. I've often thought, during the height of excitement of the dogs treeing a lion, that if I were a millionaire and could do anything I wanted to do, this is exactly what I would be doing."

Shorty will retire, ending his long career with the Department, in early 1972. He and his wife aren't sure what they will do after retirement, except for one thing. Shorty will still hunt and trap. "I've been hunting and trapping all my life and I'll continue as long as I'm physically able," he says. Shorty also plans to do more writing — articles and, maybe, even some fiction.

"And, I've been corresponding with this fellow in Venezuela," Shorty says with a far-away look in his eyes. "I've got a chance to fly down there and take my dogs and do some jaguar hunting."

When The Frost Is On The Windshield

When the frost is on the windshield
And I am snoozing in the sack
With the little wife so snug and warm
Close up again my back.

I hate to think of gettin up
I'd much rather stay in bed
Till all the frost has disappeared
And I see the sun instead.

But if you're poor and have to work
To try and made ends meet
You've gotta rise and start the day
Without this extra heat.

Sometimes I wish I'd never heard
of Reily and his plot
Of Golden -rods and foder-shocks
And all that tommy-rot.

I'd much prefer the weather warm
When I rise to meet my needs
Why can't it stay the way it was
When they were plantin pumkin seeds.

by Shortfellow

Best Top Dog

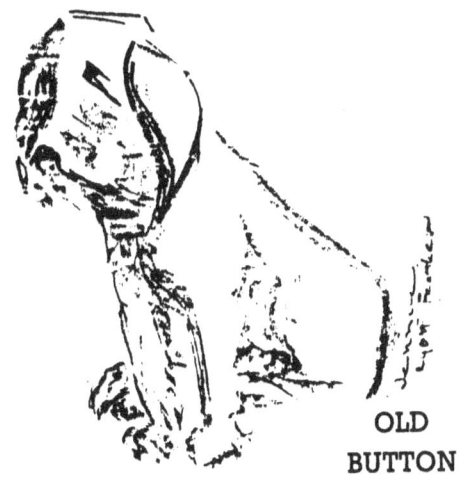

OLD
BUTTON

. . . he was a Black and Tan, Walker hound who learned to do parlor tricks to perfection with my daughter, Jennie, during the first year of his life.

. . . I believe this early training with a "natural-born -teacher" made it easy for me to teach Button the ways and life of a trapper-hunter . . . at once I marveled at his intelligence and learned to trust his judgement.

. . . and "when I get to heaven, first thing I'll do, is grab my horn and blow for Old Button."

Illustrated by Charles La Salle

SHOOTING
IN THE DARK

as told to ELLIOTT S. BARKER

BARKER SPEAKING: Trapping coyotes and hunting mountain lions in New Mexico's rough country had been Shorty Lyon's job for a long time before I retired from my post as New Mexico state game warden. Shorty is still at it.

We got together a while back to swap stories. His lonely trips as a state predator-control man always produced some good ones. This time he'd just returned from that awful cave-pocked country north of the San Francisco River, where he'd risked his hide in a dare-devil lion chase.

In all the years I was his boss, Shorty never misrepresented anything to me, and this is the way he told of his latest adventure:

A long about February 1, the north side of Apache National Forest, where I was trapping coyotes, froze up so tight I couldn't do any good. So I knocked off trapping and went to lion hunting.

A rancher, Fred Foote, and I followed a medium-size lion two days with the thermometer hitting 18 to 20° below zero at night and not getting much warmer in daytime, and finally caught him. I tried to carry the lion to camp on Lupie, a bay mare mule I bought last summer. She bucked both of us off and bunged me up considerable but luckily didn't break anything.

Next day it started storming again and I decided I'd better get out of there while I could. I tore up my tire chains in the snow and like to never made the 75-mile trip back to Mogollon. I finally had to leave my house trailer seven miles from home.

I tried to hunt around there a few days but didn't do any good so I decided to pack into the Goat Basin country, where lions had been reported killing a lot of game and some cattle.

I'd just got me a six-month-old black-and-tan hound I called Minnie Bell to go with old Slobber and I wanted to try her out. You remember Slobber, I used to call him Red till he got a mouthful of porcupine quills that made him slobber all over everything for a long time. After that I just called him Slobber.

Ozie, that two-year-old bloodhound I had, jumped out of the pick-up two years ago and got dragged to death before I knew it. I sure felt bad about that. Then you remember that speckled hound I got from Gilson that I called Blue? Well, sir, last December he and Slobber treed a lion in a bushy tree that leaned out over a 60-foot cliff. Before I could get to them, those darned dogs climbed right up that leaning tree and started fighting the lion. They both fell off. Blue hit on his back in the rocks below and died in just a little while. Old Slobber was lucky; he hit some green tree limbs that checked his fall and he landed on his feet. Slobber is seven years old now and is sure a good hound, but a fellow needs another one or two to go with him.

That Goat Basin country north of the Frisco River is awful rough, but I reckon that's why lions like it. There are caves in and under the cliffs, lots of them, big ones and little one, all kinds. Some are over 100 feet deep with ceiling 30 or 40 feet high. Many of the big ones have old Indian cliff-dwelling signs in them. No roads in there. Some of it's horseback country, lots of it you can't begin to ride through. Even afoot, you and your dogs both are always getting rimmed off.

The Holliman Ranch is as close as you can get to it with a truck, so I unloaded my pack outfit there. I got even with Lupie for throwing me off by loading her heavy with a 10-day supply of dog feed, grain for her and Tony, and my camp outfit. I rode Tony, my saddle horse. He's 15 now but still gets you there and gets you back.

Next day I rode Lupie out from my Goat Basin camp to look for lion sign. I missed a dim trail I meant to follow and got rimmed off between cliffs on the side of a box canyon. I was on the verge of turning back when I saw a big cave under the upper cliff on ahead and decided to investigate it. The place was steep and rocky with high rimrocks above and a cliff that dropped 60 feet straight off below. Lupie's tops in rough country, but this stuff stopped her. I tied Lupie to a big rock right there, where there was only three feet of level ground above the precipice for her to stand on. I reckon I shouldn't have left her there, but I thought I'd be gone only a few minutes. It didn't work out that way.

I had to climb up the hill to the cave under the cliffs and Slobber and Minnie Bell followed me. First thing I saw up there was a fresh lion scrape and the tracks of a big lion in the dust.

The tracks were leading out of the cave.

Slobber sniffed at the tracks and tested the scrape. His tail began to wag, his head came up, and he let out a bellow that roared in the cave and echoed across the canyon. He took off around the hillside as fast as he could go, baying like mad. You know, that six-month-old Minnie Bell took off after him, doing her level best to make as much noise as he was.

The track was smoking hot and I tried to keep up but didn't have a chance. Those hounds went up and down the hill, in and out of caves and cracks. On the side of the box canyon sometimes the barking and baying would echo so loud that I couldn't tell where it came from, then the hounds would go in a cave and I couldn't hear them at all. It was a wild chase but it didn't last long. Soon they went down over a cliff and cornered the lion in a big cave.

I scrambled around even with them on the ledge above and could tell by their muffled voices that they still had him at bay. I scrambled and scooted and half fell down through a break in the cliffs to get to them. The cave was sure a big one. The main room L-shaped, about 75 feet each way, and the roof was 30 feet high in places. The branch of the cave that went straight back closed down until the ceiling and floor almost met and then opened up and sloped on back for another 60 feet.

Well, sir, by now the dogs had backed the lion into that far room. I could hear the cat spitting and growling, and Slobber was making big talk right to its face. Minnie Bell was backing him up but not so bold. I was sure afraid Slobber would go too close and get himself torn to pieces.

Slobber was too valuable to risk losing and I knew all hell couldn't call him off, so I decided I'd have to crawl on in and do what he expected me to. He'd done his part.

Sure, I was scared. I couldn't hardly see anything back in there. I was afraid to light a match, for the lights and shadows might confuse that old hound and cause him to get too close to those terrible sharp claws and teeth. Slobber had been faithful to me and was the only trained lion dog I had left. I just didn't aim to lose him. But the way it was he might crowd the old lion too much and get hurt bad, for he was talking awful big. Scared or not, there wasn't but one thing left for me to do, so I gritted my teeth and started.

Mind you, the lion was about 140 feet from the mouth of the cave, separated from me by a place where the ceiling was low and the floor humped up, leaving a space so narrow I had to crawl through it. So there wasn't hardly any light back there where they were. After I got through the first tight place I could stand up for a little way, then it got tight again. So I slid and crawled on back. As I went, cautious-like, my eyes got accustomed to the dark. I could make out the forms of animals ahead but couldn't tell one from t'other.

Minnie Bell was making a lot of noise backing Slobber up but she wasn't quite as brave as he was. Neither was I. Finally I crawled a few feet farther and crouched there. I had my six-shooter, and old-time .32/20 Smith & Wesson, out and ready. At last I could tell which was the lion and which was Slobber but that was all.

When Slobber found I was coming in close he doubled his baying and crowded the cat even more, jumping back when the lion's paw lashed out at him. The lion was spitting and growling and I expected him to come out of that cave in spite of me and the dogs.

When I was sure I wouldn't hit Slobber, I leveled my six-shooter near as I could guess at the lions' head and cut loose with five shots as fast as I could get them off. Then, by golly, I scrambled out of there in high.

Soon as I got back where I could see better I reloaded my six-gun and crawled back to the dungeon. But before I got to them, Slobber had quit baying and I could hear him roughing up the lion. The cat was stone-dead. One bullet had hit him in the neck and one right over the eye, and I'd made three misses. Probably the first two shots got him and when he slumped I overshot him. He was about the biggest lion I ever killed and so fat he was pot-bellied.

Well, sir, now that it was all over I felt a little shaky. I had a time dragging him out of that cave. Ever try to drag a big lion uphill in the dark on your hands and knees? Well, don't. I finally made it. Then, there at the mouth of the cave, I skinned him. Carrying the hide, I headed up, over, and around the rugged country to where I'd left Lupie tied.

When I came in sight my heart sank, for some way that dang-
ed mule had turned around and got astraddle of the halter
rope with her front and hind feet both. Her rump was tight
against the big rock she was tied to, and her head was drawn
down between her front legs. Imagine her there in that fix,
only two or three feet from a 60-foot precipice! If she struggled
any, she was sure to fall and roll over the cliff. I knew she was
afraid of lion scent and I reeked with it. How I was going to get
her out of this, I didn't know.

I dropped the lion skin and kept on slowly, talking to her
quiet-like. "Whoa, Lupie, whoa. Don't move, Lupie. Whoa
now, whoa!"

A mule seems to have more sense about not getting hurt than
horses, and I reckon Lupie realized she was in mortal danger,
for, in spite of my bloody hands and lion smell, she let me ease
up to her and unbuckle the halter strap to free her. Some mule,
that Lupie.

When I got back to camp safely with my mule, my dogs, my
own hide, and with a big lion to go on my monthly report, I felt
like I'd been mighty lucky.

I vowed I'd never go back to hunt that kind of country again,
but you know how it is. A couple of days later I got to thinking
that if I set some traps near the lion's carcass I'd sure to pick up
a bobcat or two. So I went back, but this time I tied Lupie in a
safe place with a short rope so she couldn't get astraddle of it.

Well, sir, when I got to the lion carcass at the mouth of the
cave I was sure surprised to find there'd been another lion
there. Tracks in the cave dust looked like a female's and darned
if she hadn't eaten a good meal or two off of the old boy's carcass — two thirds of his hams and a big place out of the back.
Did you know they'd eat their own kind? Well, she sure had.

We took her trail and had a lot of trouble getting out of the
canyon. Boulders, rocks and cliffs made it a tough trail to
follow, but we finally topped out. I was up on a bluff and the
hounds were working down below it when suddenly I saw the
lion jump and run. She was across a rough side draw and
below me. It was long range for the scope-sighted .22 Special I
carry on my saddle, I took two quick shots at her — and missed. My shots confused old Slobber and he left the track and

came to me, supposing I had killed his lion. So, to get him back on the trail, I had to scramble across the rugged side canyon to get down to where I'd seen her last.

When Slobber hit that fresh trail, the race was sure on. He and Minnie Bell made the canyon echo with their bellowing, and I ran after them. When I reached the brink of the bluffs my feet felt as if they were afire. At that, I thought I hadn't been fast enough, for the noise of some falls down on the river bothered me and I couldn't hear the hounds.

After half an hour of working back and forth along the top, I heard muffled baying somewhere in the bluffs below me. I finally found a way down to where Slobber was barking treed and looking up into the cliffs.

At first I saw nothing and thought the old hound must be mistaken, that the lion had given him the slip. Then away up there in the bluffs I saw her peeking around a point of rocks, so I could just see one eye and one ear. I tried a shot at the tiny target, but darned if I didn't miss again. She disappeard and I was afraid she'd get away by going where we couldn't follow. Slobber sure acted disgusted with me.

I climbed around the rough cliffs and, at last, was able to crawl out on a high place where I could see quite a lot of the bluffs and shelves and crevices beyond and below me. I watched for a long time. Just when I concluded she'd given us the slip for sure, I saw her. That lioness had fooled me; she'd moved quite a ways and was much lower on the cliffs than I had expected her to be. Now she was crouching, getting herself ready to make a long jump across a wide crevice.

I shot and hit her just as she started to leap. She jumped anyway but didn't make it and fell. It was 50 feet or more down to the next shelf in the bluffs and she hit hard. I could see her where she landed on the rock shelf, struggling to get to her feet again. I let off two more shots that finished her.

For a while I thought I'd just have to leave her there, but I finally found a way to get down and skin her out. I rolled the carcass over the lowest of the cliffs, a sheer drop of 70 feet or more, and it hit right at the edge of the river.

Now the excitement was over and all I had to do was carry that lion hide up a few cliffs to where I'd left Lupie.

When at long last I got back to camp, I decided I'd had enough of it for a while. All the same, what Lupie, Slobber, Minnie Bell, and I had got done would save a lot of game and livestock.

Come down sometime and we'll go back in there. The End.

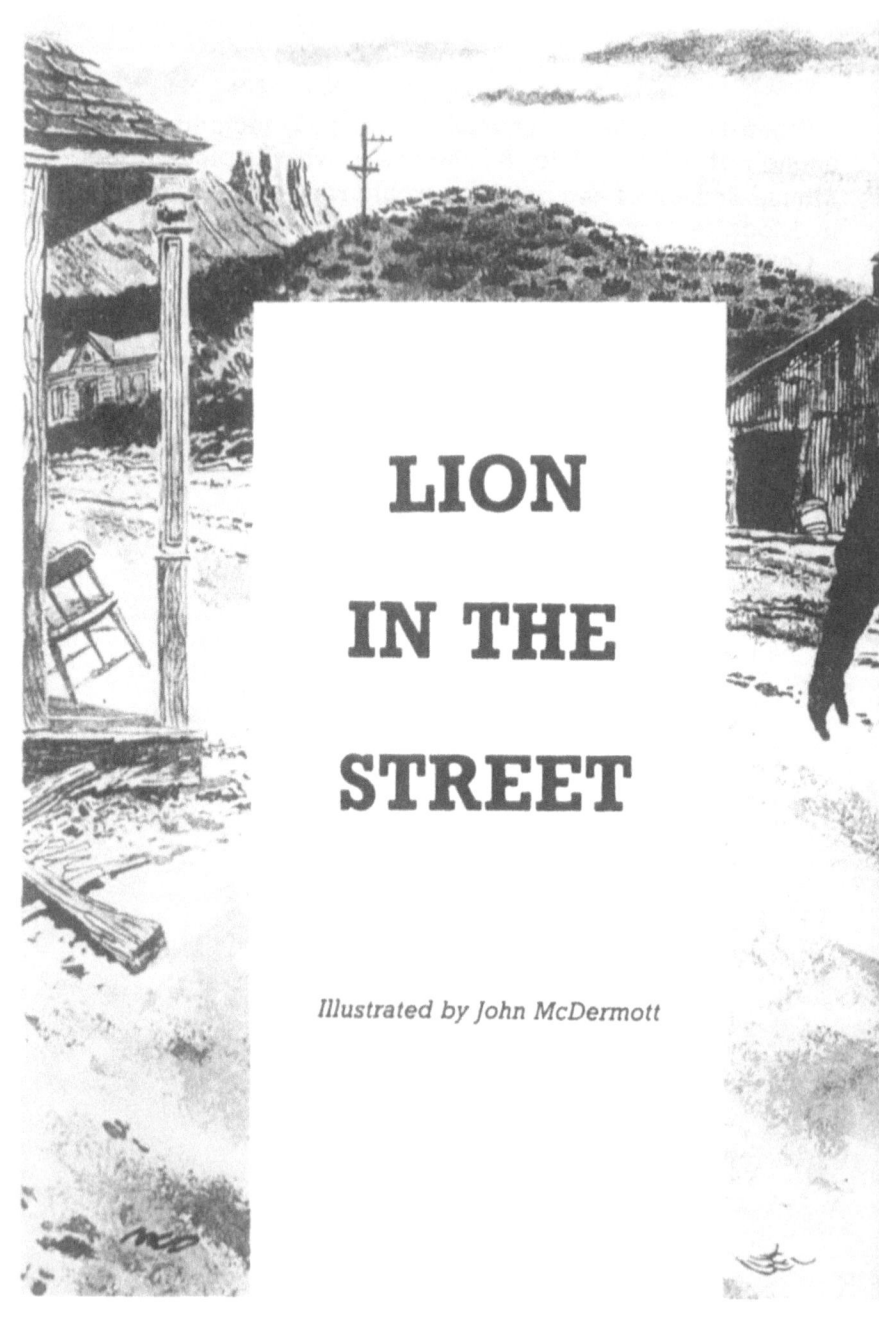

LION

IN THE

STREET

Illustrated by John McDermott

I've killed quite a few mountain lions in my time, but this one was the first to come out in the open and ask for it.

I am T. J. Lyon. I live at Mogollon, New Mexico. I am a government lion hunter, and I believe I've got a story that is a little unusual, to say the least, about a lion I killed in the town of Mogollon a few years ago.

In order to get this story across, for I hope to make it entertaining, I am going to have to describe some places and get away from the lion once in a while. But I understand when a fellow starts to read a lion story he wants to read more about lions than anything else, so I'll try not to stay away from the lion too long at any one time.

To begin with, I was over on the New Mexico-Arizona state line at a place called Alma Mesa, with a friend of mine, Frank Lyons. Frank is not related to me, but we're awful good friends. Frank is a rough-and-tough cowboy who runs quite a spread over there for John McKeen, and he sure likes to hunt lion too.

Frank and I had been really hitting the trails trying our best to find a lion for about a week. We had worn ourselves out, and two or three good horses, and our dogs, and we just hadn't had a bit of luck. I'd given up, and left in the evening in my jeep. I had my top lion dog, Old Button, with me and we'd headed back for Mogollon.

Mogollon is a picturesque little town high up in the Mogollon Mountains. At one time it was quite a busy mining camp for gold and silver. When I came there some 20 years ago, there were 2,000 or 3,000 people living there. Now it's a ghost town. Some people who live there don't want you to call it a ghost town. But I guess it's almost a ghost town anyway.

Now I would like to tell you what was going on at Mogollon just a little while before I got there. The town is scattered out up and down Silver Creek Canyon, which is real steep, and the buildings are built right along the bottom. That's the only level place to make a building. In fact some of those steep places had to be leveled before you could build, and then most the buildings touched or very near touched the mountainside at the back end.

There's an elderly lady who lives up one of these canyons, and she is quite a person. She is Mrs. Sill Gamblin. I guess she's been there almost as long as the town has, which is really a long time. Mrs. Gamblin is quite an observer, and I guess you'd say she has led more or less of a monotonous life there. But she manages to know what's going on, and she didn't miss this lion either.

She looked out the door this evening just about sundown, and to her surprise down the middle of the road walked a mountain lion — a big one. Well, there wasn't anyone that lived in easy hollering distance of Mrs. Gamblin. My folks lived up on the hill about a mile from there, and the next closest neighbor was a quarter of a mile away.

Mrs. Gamblin felt like she ought to do something; she couldn't just watch this lion walk by. That's kind of hard to do. She didn't know anything else to do so she hollered just as loud as she could. Well, when she yelled this lion stopped and looked back at her instead of running, as most lions usually do if they hear a human voice or see anyone. But as this story goes on, you will see that this is a most unusual lion.

Mrs. Gamblin said that after she'd hollered and the lion looked at her a minute, it then started walking on down the road. So she hollered again, and the lion stopped and looked back again. This was repeated three or four times, but the lion never swerved from its course. It walked right on down the middle of the road, across a little bridge, and went on down toward town.

Down in what we call the main part of town where the tall buildings are, two stories some of them, James Wray, the postmaster of Mogollon, was working late getting the mail up in the post office. Wray had a little Irish terrier dog with him. He thought the world of it, and it was a real smart, nice, little dog.

The dog was outside in the street and we never will know exactly what happened, whether the lion jumped onto the dog or the dog jumped onto the lion. But the way this old lion looked to me, hungry and beat up and all, I imagine that it jumped the dog, probably with the intention of killing and eating it, because the lion must have been very hungry and getting desperate for food.

The first thing Wray knew about the lion's presence was that he heard a terrible fight and commotion, a growling and carrying on outside. So he rushed out to see what it was all about. When he got to where he could see there in the dusk a huge yellow animal had his little dog down and was just — well in fact it was killing it. Of course, at the time Wray just thought it was a huge yellow dog that had his little dog down.

But, as I said, Wray thought a lot of his little dog and he wasn't going to have any other dog eat it up like that, no matter how big it was. So he just ran out and started kicking it. This animal stood up to Wray after he'd kicked it as hard as he could three or four times, and it was easy to tell that it wasn't a dog. It was a mountain lion, and a huge one.

It snarled and spit at him and let him know in no uncertain terms that it was a lion, and that it was ready to take him on along with his dog if he cared to get involved.

Now I believe that right then Wray was in great danger, because this lion wasn't like a good, healthy, fat lion that runs from a hunter or a pack of dogs. On the contrary, this lion was the hunter itself, and it was out to get meat, blood, or something to eat regardless of the risk it was taking.

Of course, when Wray saw that it was a lion and in a very vicious frame of mind, he did the only thing any sane person would do under the circumstances. He ran back into the post office building.

But he didn't stay there long. Because of his devotion to his dog, he came right out.

After Wray had kicked it, the lion had left the dog and run around the corner of the two-story building. Wray supposed the lion had left, and I did too at first, after I got to the scene. Wray picked up his little dog and took her into the post office.

He'd just been there a few minutes when I came along in my jeep. By this time it was getting quite dark. Wray heard the jeep coming and he ran out in the street and stopped me. He said, "Shorty, a big mountain lion just killed my dog and ran around behind the store there!"

Now I knew that Wray was a reliable man, but for a mountain lion to come down to the main part of town looking for trouble, that didn't make sense. Or I thought it didn't make sense, rather. So I was kind of cautious, and I said "Wray, I know you think you're telling the truth, but surely a mountain lion wasn't here."

"Look at the blood," he said. I looked, and there were great pools of blood, some as big as a tub, in the road. So I said, "Well, something sure happened here."

I hadn't let Old Button out yet. As I explained before, Old Button was my top lion dog, and I had him with me in the jeep. I started to open the door and turn him loose, but Wray insisted that I come into the post office and look at his little dog. He told me that he thought she was dead. So I went in and took a look at Wray's dog. I told him she wasn't dead just then, but she was in a terrible state from loss of blood and probably would die, which she did later.

"I'm anxious to get after this lion, Wray," I said. I started to go out then, and I noticed how dark it was, so I asked him if I might borrow a flashlight. He handed me one, and I went outside then and let Button out of the jeep.

I thought I had a good trail, and that Button would pick it up and eventually tree the lion probably a half a mile or so down the canyon, maybe a mile. That's the way a good lion trail turns out sometimes. But sometimes you don't even get the lion.

At first Button was confused by so much blood from this little dog of Wray's, and he was slow getting started. But after he'd been smelling around for a minute, I guess the wind blew the lion's scent to him. Anyway, he just bristled up and away he went around the corner. To my surprise that lion was right there, just a few feet from where Wray had seen it.

It had gone into an old shed. Well, sir, Button went into this shed and I'm telling you, business picked up! That lion certainly knew he'd found a different kind of a dog from the one that he'd cleaned up in front of the store. The fight was so furious, and they were so tangled up, that when I'd flash my light in I couldn't tell which was which, but soon they came out of that shed and ran up on top of a two-story building, where the building almost touched the mountains in the back.

I don't know whether any other lion hunter has ever experienced chasing mountain lions at night over the tops of store buildings or not, but I'm telling you, boys, it's quite a deal. I would flash my light and see them dart here, and I'd flash it and see them dart there, and I never could get a shot, looked like. Once in a while they'd stop and fight, but it would be where I was afraid to get in because they'd be in such close quarters.

This didn't last too long. They came out on top of a two-story building that had some chicken wire nailed up there. The lady that had run the store there years ago, when the camps were running, had put the chicken wire up to keep her grandchildren from falling off.

Of course the lion didn't realize what this chicken wire was, and it jumped into it a time or two. Button jumped right after it. They were so close that I didn't dare to shoot as I was afraid of hurting my dog.

After the third run into this chicken wire, it broke down, and lion and dog fell below in a kind of a deep ditch off behind the store. The lion jumped right straight back out, and this was the first chance I got for a shot. I had the light on and I could tell by its tail that it was the lion instead of my dog, so I took a quick snapshot. I don't think I even got the gun to my shoulder. I really don't remember, but I know I missed the lion.

It ran right straight up the mountain toward some high bluffs, up on what we call Fanny Hill, above the town. Button was just a few seconds getting out of there. He had to go a few feet down below to where he could get out, but he was out and after that lion in nothing flat.

I started off the way they went, of course, as hard as I could run, but I was pretty slow compared with that big cat and Button. I'd hardly got started when I heard them coming back. They'd run to the foot of some high bluffs, and the old lion saw it couldn't scale them on account of them being so high, so it had turned and started back.

I knew of some more high bluffs at the lower end of Mogollon, so I ran and waved my flashlight, hoping to turn the lion that way. I don't know whether I had anything to do with it, or if Button did it all by himself, but we got the lion out on those high bluffs at the end of town.

When I got down there I went to work around the bluffs with my flashlight, and I wasn't long in finding the lion. Button had it backed out on a little narrow ledge where it could barely stand, and he was right up in its face fighting. It was spitting and snarling and striking at him. They were making so much noise defying each other that I guess Button couldn't hear me very well, or else he didn't care. Anyhow, I scolded and scolded, and I thought he never would get back to where I'd be safe shooting the lion. But he finally backed up a few feet, and I held the flashlight beam on the lion and shot it.

It fell off below the bluff, perhaps 100 feet, a long way anyway, and straight down. Well, I listened, it being so dark down below in Silver Creek that I couldn't see. I listened with the idea that if I hadn't killed it dead, and it jumped to run, I could hear which way it was going and help Button to find the trail.

I didn't listen very long, because when the lion fell off that bluff Button left there. The next thing I heard down below me was Button chewing and shaking it. It was dead.

I made my way down to them and looked the lion over. I found it was a huge female that must have surely come out of old Mexico or from way in the south somewhere. Her hair was short and coarse, not like that of lions of cooler climates. They have longer and finer hair than the southern lions. She was footsore and poor. Her teeth were worn off, she smelled like skunk, and had several porcupine quills in her. She had a lot of old scars, many that were just recently healed.

I think she'd really been having some trouble, and had been on a long, hard trip. She had wound up in Mogollon, and was determined to get something to eat. She was about at her rope's-end. I think she would have been a very dangerous lion to fool with, especially a little child. I am thankful that James Wray's little boys weren't playing out in the street that evening, as they often did at mail time, for it might have been a much worse tragedy than it was.

Well, I started back up the street of Mogollon. The lion was too heavy for me to carry. Button was walking along by my side when I met some people that lived down below where we'd jumped the lion. They were Mrs. Nell and Ace Johnson. They saw that I didn't have a lion on my shoulder, so they said, "Too bad it got away."

"She didn't get away," I said. "She's lying back there in the creek."

"Well let's go back and get her," they said. So we went back and loaded her in their pick-up and brought her on up to the post office.

Wray was out in the street, and he said, "Shorty, you don't mean to tell me that first shot you fired right here in the back of the store was at that lion."

"It sure was," I said. "She never left here. She was planning to stick around and eat your little dog. I'm sure that's what she had in mind."

Well, this poor little dog died of its wounds. I took Wray and his dog in my jeep on up to his house. He lived a couple miles up above in one of the canyons.

I had to pass Mrs. Gramblin's house on the way up, the lady that had first seen the lion coming down the road into Mogollon. I was driving pretty steady and got by her place on the way up. But she recognized my jeep, and on the way back I saw a light bobbing across the bridge at her house. I was afraid for her, afraid she might slip on the ice. It was that kind of weather, pretty icy, and Mrs. Gramblin is elderly. So I slowed down and stopped.

"It's about time you was getting here," she said. "What's the matter, Mrs. Gamblin?" I asked.

36

"There was a great big lion just come down this road, just about dark," she said.

I first let on to her like I didn't believe it, but she was so excited that I couldn't do that very long. So I told her everything that had happened, and I showed her the lion in the back of my jeep.

Well, I don't know much else to say except this is about the first time I ever had a lion just come and ask for it, and I've caught a lot of lions. And if this isn't an unusual lion story, I just don't know where you'd find one. The End.

Illustrated by Morris Gollub

VERY BIG LION

*Un leon grande, the old Mexican called him. He
was a big lion, sure enough, but it wasn't just his
size that scared me.*

I notice that educated writers often start telling a story with
the most exciting part, maybe opening at the point where
a tiger has just gobbled up a native and is about to have
the white hunter for dessert.

I guess a man writing that way would start my story with the
scrap in Charlie Munns Canyon, where I was standing in the
middle of a fight between my two dogs and a big male lion that
was wounded and mad. My favorite dog, old Slobber, grabbed the lion from behind, and I saw the flash of white as the
cougar extended his inch-long claws in a swipe that jerked
some hide and hair off the dog. Lucky for Slobber, the blow
wasn't solid enough for the claws to sink in deep.

Two streams of blood the size of a pencil were spurting from
the lion's head, then spraying to each side as steady and even
as a lawn sprinkler. The dogs would charge the lion, then it
would rush the dogs. Me, I was jumping around trying to get in
a shot. I was scared, worried about my hounds, and cussing

myself for causing the whole mess with my carelessness.

I started out on this hunt from the abandoned mining town of Mogollon, in southwestern New Mexico. My home is there and I work in the surrounding area as a government predator hunter, spending a lot of my time hunting down stock-killing mountain lions.

I rode out of Mogollon on Lupie, my saddle mule, at first sign of daylight this summer morning. The fresh coolness of a rain the day before was something to make a man real pleased that he was among the living, going hunting on a good sure-footed mule, with some dogs that were more interested in finding a lion track than anything else. Maybe there's a better feeling, but I don't know about it.

There are several old buildings in Mogollon, and a few people who still call it home. But as we rode through I didn't see any lights. It was still too early for most people to be up.

We rode up Silver Creek and Whitewater Creek. This is real lion country, some of the best I know. The only trouble is the the rough bluffs on the Whitewater side cause you to lose more lions than you catch. If a cat gets to these bluffs, it has a big advantage over a man or his dogs. The lion can make tremendous jumps across crevices that force a man or dog to detour. I've seen lions make leaps of 30 to 40 feet, and watched them go up cliffs so straight up and down you wouldn't think anything could climb them.

Yet we sometimes get lions here on this Whitewater ridge, and I keep thinking today will be the time. So my hopes were plenty high as I turned down the main ridge.

The dogs were out ahead testing the brush, which is the way they often pick up the scent. Low brush touching the lion as it passes through sometimes holds the scent better than the ground or rocks.

I had three dogs with me. My top hound, Slobber, is a solid red dog out of a pack raised by Frank Armijo of Jewett Gap, New Mexico. Frank, who is a noted lion hunter, got some of his first hounds from the penitentiary in Santa Fe. My second experienced dog, Minnie Bell, has ancestors that hunted cougars and bears with the famous mountain man Ben Lilly. The third hound on this trip was a little spotted female just old enough to start learning the ropes. Her name is Spot, and she, like the rest of my dogs, has quite a mixture of hound blood — blood-hound, bluetick, redbone, black and tan, and Walker. About the only sure thing about the ancestry of my dogs is that they're 100 percent hound, with no crosses with any kind of dog not bred to follow a scent trail.

You don't find a lion trail every time you go out, and you don't catch a lion each time you do find a trail. But if a man's got a drop of hunting blood in him, he sure does thrill to the sight of seeing his dogs out there trying to find lion scent.

At intervals along this main ridge there are saddles where small canyons come up from either side of the ridge. These saddles are extra-good places to strike a trail, as the lions regularly travel through such gaps. Often a male lion will leave his scent in a little pile of pine needles he scrapes up. It notifies any interested females that he's in the area.

There's a lot of lion traffic along this main ridge, and it has scent beds at intervals. These scent beds are like bulletin boards where the cats leave notes for one another. The male is the only one that leaves the scrape marks, but I believe the female also leaves her scent at the scent beds.

We had passed two of these saddles and were about a mile and a half down the main ridge when we came into the third saddle. It had been about a month since I last hunted here, but I noticed a new scrape in the pine needles before the dogs got to it. Of course it could still be too old to be of any significance, but I sure was watching old Slobber when he trotted up to that little mound and made his inspection.

His tail started wagging just a little bit out on the end. The wagging quickened fast, until his tail was a blur. Then he let out a roar that said "Lion, and no mistake about it!"

Minnie Bell took long leaps getting to him. She downed her head and went through about the same act that Slobber had. The pup, Spot, joined in.

They all got real busy there for a minute, circling around to be sure where the lion had gone. Then they lined out down the main ridge, going fast and doing plenty of talking.

I said to Lupie, "Well, here's where you pay for some of th oats you've been eating," and away we went.

41

It was still pretty early and the ground was damp. That combination makes for strong scent trails, so I couldn't be sure if the lion had been along in the early part of the night or whether he'd just passed.

But I soon realized one thing; if I was going to stay in hearing of the dogs, I'd have to do some fast riding. So I did, getting pretty reckless and Western at times. Lupie is good at getting over rough ground fast, but the dogs were getting farther ahead by the minute.

They kept right down the main ridge. That was a break for me. If they'd turned off to the left, toward Whitewater Creek, I'd have had to quit my mule and go on afoot, because not even sure-footed Lupie can pack a man down through those bluffs.

I passed two more scent beds and saw fresh scrapes at them. I knew now I was after a large male lion.

The dogs were soon out of hearing. This is bad, because there's always the chance that the dogs will tree and you won't be able to find them. You don't want to let them down. It's your part of the deal to shoot the lion out after they tree it. There's also a chance that the dogs will corner the lion on a bluff or on the ground and get seriously hurt or killed because you're not there to help them.

I came to a place where a big ridge ran off from the main ridge into Whitewater, on my left. After looking around for a few minutes, I found sign where the dogs had turned down this ridge.

I hustled Lupie down it for half a mile, then suddenly heard the dogs again. They seemed to be straight on down the ridge and still far ahead of me. After riding some more, I stopped to listen again. This time they were much closer, and I could tell they had the cat treed or bayed.

When I got to them, they were on top of one of the worst bluffs in this whole jumbled area. Old Slobber was peering down at 40 acres of stuff that you'd have to see to believe. It was cut up by bluffs that were more than 100 feet straight up and down. There were wide crevices, benches, and caves, with a little brush growing here and there. It was a ideal place for a lion to hide.

Slobber said, "he went down in there, boss," the dog was

barking at the brink of a 20-foot drop-off.

I tied Lupie to a stunted juniper tree, took my gun, and got the dogs to follow me to a place where it looked as if we might be able to get down.

We made it, after a lot of work, but the lion had run 100 yards and jumped a wide crevice that stopped us again.

The dogs ran back and forth and did a lot of barking. They sure wanted across that crack in the bluff, but it was an impossible jump for them. Then I saw a place where I might climb high up, come down, and maybe get across. I felt sure the lion was close, somewhere in this mess. I took a small rope and made a sling for my rifle so I'd have both hands free. Leaving the dogs there, I started climbing.

The dogs set up a loud fuss. They wanted to go too. They knew as well as I that Mr. Longtail was hiding somewhere near, and they wanted to help find him. But there wasn't anything I could do but leave the dogs. I did well to get myself around and over these broken cliffs. At times I took chances I knew I shouldn't, but all lion hunters do that.

It was about 11 o'clock now and the sun was bearing down with a close, humid kind of heat. There were big thunderheads in the distance, and I could hear far-off thunder. I kept working around, looking the best I could into the crevices and on the ledges.

All this time the dogs were complaining and trying to find a way to get to me. Part of the time they couldn't see me, and this worried them even more.

At last I got the notion that probably the lion had gone down through the bluffs to Whitewater Creek. With this idea in mind, I went back to the dogs, got them bunched and close to me, and started picking out a way down. At times I had to help them down off places that were too high for them to jump.

I got to the foot of the main bluffs, when all at once the dogs all bawled and ran at the same time — headed toward the bottom of the canyon.

I ran a few steps after them, looking for tracks. When I reached a small patch of clear soil I saw that the tracks in it were going up instead of down. The dogs were tracking the lion the wrong way.

When this happens it calls for quick, drastic action. I know one way to make my dogs come to me in a hurry. It's sort of a double-cross, but good for all concerned. I started yelling at the top of my voice and firing into the air. The dogs, thinking I'd seen the lion, came charging back up the mountain at full speed. I ran the way the lion had gone, waving and shouting.

This got them going the right way on the trail, and it was red-hot. That old lion had been holed up right under us all the time we'd been looking in the right place, we probably would have seen him run out ahead of us as we scrambled down the bluffs.

There was a little canyon that ran from the bluffs up to the top of the main ridge. It was steep, narrow and choked with brush. Huge bolders, some of them as big as a house, were scattered along the bottom.

The lion had run up this canyon to the top, and the dogs lost no time in getting up there also. They sure made the mountains ring with their baying. If a man had needed anything to urge him on, this would have done it.

I was scrambling up through the brush and rocks at my best speed, which seemed mighty slow to me. Before I had to stop for breath the first time, the dogs had already gone over the top of the main ridge and out of hearing.

At times like this, I wish I was young again. But wishing doesn't help — I'm almost 50 and several pounds too heavy. So all I could do was stop and pant when I seemed to be on the verge of a heat stroke.

By the time I reached the ridgetop, sweat was running into my eyes until I couldn't see and I could feel a steady trickle going down my spine. My temples were pounding and lungs burning. You'd think a man who's killed a lot of lions would have more sense, but this man hasn't.

The first sound I heard after I got on top was the pup, Spot. She was up on the side of Charley Munns Canyon, which heads on the other side of the ridge. It's a cool, timbered canyon named after the Charley Munns mine at the mouth of it.

Spot barked again, and she sounded like a pup that was really bad scared. This worried me, because I couldn't hear the old dogs. Two silent dogs and a scared pup — that suggest all kinds of trouble. I called to Spot but she wouldn't come to me, and there was too much thick brush for me to see her.

I was climbing toward her when old Slobber barked treed right down under me near the bottom of this little canyon. Believe me, it was a welcome sound. I wasted no time getting down to where he was.

He and Minnie had the lion in a big spruce, and Minnie was silent for the simple reason that she was too tired to bark. She had a litter of pups at home that were still nursing, and I wouldn't have brought her along on this hunt if she hadn't made such a fuss when I started to leave her behind. Slobber was almost as hot and tired as Minnie Bell, and I was far from being cool and rested myself.

The lion had gone up 60 to 70 feet. He was sitting on a big limb, and panting hard for his breaths, just like the rest of us.

I called and called Spot, but couldn't get her to come down to the tree. She would only bark that scared bark. I believe this lion had made a pass at her, and probably came close to getting her. This really put the fear in her, and now she wanted no part of him. I tried to go to her, but she ran from me. I gave up on getting her in on the kill.

When I thought I was rested enough to shoot straight, I steadied the rifle against a little pine tree and took careful aim at the lion's head, my sights on the center of his forehead. That's a dead shot if you hit where you aim.

I was using a .22 Special with a scope sight that wasn't mounted right. The trouble with the scope showed up some days earlier, when Howard (Doggie) Jones and I were using the rifle to shoot rabbits on his ranch near Luna, New Mexico. The scope is old and worn, and one end of it was held with tape that had gradually worked loose. Doggie and I used the iron sights beneath the scope to kill the rabbits I wanted for dog food, and I hadn't got around to tighting the scope and sighting it in again.

So I was using the open iron sights for my shot at the lion. They are fairly accurate, but this time I wasn't seeing them quite right. They seemed to have fuzz on them. Nevertheless, I figured the shot was easy enough that I'd kill the lion dead with one bullet.

Well, at the crack of the gun, I didn't have to figure any longer. I knew I'd made a mess of it.

Instead of falling out, the lion turned his head down, ran down the tree trunk till he was 15 feet off the ground, then jumped out over the dogs and hit running. I could see blood spurting out of his head as he ran. Of course the dogs were right on his tail.

The dogs treed him again about 200 yards below, and he climbed pretty high. A steady jet of blood from his head splattered down through the limbs and pine needles.

I felt guilty for making such a mess of what should have been a quick, clean kill, so I hurried my second shot.

At the crack of the gun, there was a repeat performance of that scene at the first tree. The lion came down the trunk — not backing down as a bear has to do, but running headfirst as easy as a squirrel. It's a fairly common lion stunt, and I've seen them do it several times before, yet it always amazes me.

There was a steep bank beside this tree, and the cat tried to climb it. That's when Slobber grabbed him by the haunch as he climbed. Then came the action I described at the first of the story. The lion was spouting blood and scattering dogs. I was real busy too, first trying to get close to the cougar to get in a shot, then trying to get away from him. He'd charge the dogs each time they pressed too close, and they'd come running to me with the big cat right behind them.

I suppose it was the dogs he was after mostly, but I was afraid of him, big as he was and fighting for his life. Any big animal is dangerous when cornered and hurt, and a big cat is probably more dangerous than most on account of its fighting equipment. A cougar could kill a man with either its teeth or claws, and it handles both with a speed that scares you.

Well, we gave and took ground there for three or four minutes. The lion was getting weak from loss of blood by then, and old Slobber took some awful close risks in order to bite him a few times. Finally the cat turned from us and the dogs were slow in going after him, which gave me an opening for another shot. I hit him in the back of the head and killed him.

I went back up the ridge and got my mule. Spot, the scared pup, followed me as I rode back past her toward the dead lion. But she stopped about 100 yards from the kill and wouldn't come any closer.

The lion was plenty heavy to load on my mule after he was dressed out, but I made it after doing a lot of hard lifting and grunting.

As I rode down the main street of Mogollon, the total population (about a dozen) came out to see the lion. An old Mexican looked the cat over and said, "Un leon muy grande," which in Spanish means "A very big lion."

I said, "Si, senor. It was a big lion, the biggest I ever caught."

The End.

Button broke loose and began barking right into her face. I tried desperately to grab hold of something, but there wasn't any way I could stop sliding down toward that cat. All I could do was shoot in her ear as I jumped over her.

LION IN MY LAP

Illustrated by Morris Gollub

I f you never have lived up against high mountains or in any place where you can get snowed in, you sure have missed something. Here at Mogollon, New Mexico, where I live, the road ends in the wintertime. It's a little forest road that winds around our end of Willow Mountain. It was built long ago by convict labor from Santa Fe, when a man named Bursom was superintendent of the penitentiary there. So it's called Bursom Road.

Usually this road, which climbs to about 9,000 feet, is snowed in by early December or even sooner. Of course, during the drought of the last few years we haven't had as much snow as we'd like, but I've seen the time when the road was so bad hunters couldn't get out without help from the U.S. Forest Service. We have our hunting season here about the middle of November.

There's something about country that snows in. Seems like the snow gives it a rest. People leave the place alone, and the game is on its own. To me, it's just like the country is having a good sleep. Then in spring, when you get back in, there's a certain freshness about everything that I sure appreciate, because nobody has been around there for a period of several months.

This Willow Mountain is what you might call the mother mountain of the Mogollons here at the north end. It's a great, sprawling mountain, and there are lots of places on it where you can't ride a horse. When it drops off into the head of main

49

Whitewater Creek or into Mineral Creek, the only place you can ride a horse is on a trail. It's too steep other places for a horse even to stand up.

There's a dude ranch about 18 miles back in the mountain called the Willow Creek Ranch. The people who run it try to stay there and be the last ones out. Then when it snows in to where they aren't afraid anyone will get in to bother anything, they come out. There was an old fellow, Len Shellhorn, over there, who had a bunch of horses he rented to dudes, and he was staying until the snow got too heavy and forced him out. Outside of him, there wasn't anyone in that part of the country.

The reason I'm telling this is because the lion story I'm going to tell happened during just about the last trip anybody could make back in Willow Mountain country. Hunting season was over and the hunters were out.

On this particular morning I was out early, driving a jeep with my dogs in it, looking for fresh lion tracks. At the time I was working as a lion hunter for the New Mexico Department of Game and Fish. About five or six inches of fresh snow had fallen on a pretty good snow already on the ground. I didn't take a horse because I thought if I found a lion track in horse country I could come back and get one. But I knew the chances were I'd find a track in foot country.

I was driving along Willow Mountain road and soon came across some big lion tracks. They went along the road for a way, then turned off below me.

I don't know why I keep getting so excited over lion tracks after all these years. I go just as nutty over a fresh lion track now as I did the first day I saw one. That was in Leon Canyon, south of Quemado, New Mexico, about 27 years ago. I was a poor "one-mattress Okey" at the time (a rich Okey had two mattress), trying to make a go of it on a homestead. I didn't have a dog that would trail a lion, so I did it myself for two days.

So now, instead of taking the precaution of getting the dogs started in the right direction, I just jerked the jeep door open and let them pour out. They were Slobber, then only a two-year-old; a big cur dog call Old Bob, which belonged to my son Jimmie, and Old Button. Button was my top dog.

All three fell out of the jeep and ran down the lion tracks for a way. Then Old Bob and Slobber treed at a big spruce. Button made a circle around the same tree, but he didn't bark treed.

I was looking in the jeep for some food to put in my pocket when I suddenly realized I didn't have any dogs. They'd vanished. The snow was deep and fresh around there, and when you made a track fresh snow would fall into it. So you couldn't learn anything just by looking at tracks.

The mountainside was so steep I decided not to carry a gun because I would need both hands to get along there. Instead I took my six-shooter, an old-time .32/20 Smith & Wesson, that I've killed lions with before, and put a handful of shells in my pocket. Then I went down to see what I could see about those tracks.

I found that Slobber and Bob had gone one way, and Button another. The way the snow had fallen in the tracks, I couldn't tell which was the right way. But while I was wondering what to do, I heard Button barking way down below me. He'd tracked the lion a long way off toward Mineral Creek.

Since I was figuring on Button most to tree this lion, I followed the trail he'd made. I hadn't gone far when I saw where the lion had walked under a big spruce tree. I saw a plain track and knew that Button had gone the right way and the other dogs had gone the wrong way. They'd taken the back trail.

This made me feel good. I hurried right along, once in a while stepping on a slick, dead branch under the snow and sitting down hard. It was tough walking. I was using my hands almost as much as my feet, grabbing onto trees and brush as I went. The snow was wet and the trees were just covered with it. At first, a little of it would get down my collar and I'd try to brush it out, but soon I just couldn't keep it out so quit paying attention to it. Now and then I'd touch a tree that was bent over with snow, and when I did it was like pulling a trigger. The tree would fly up and a shower of snow would come down all over me.

By the time I was halfway down the mountain I was as wet as if you'd held me in a tank of ice water. But I was moving along so fast the cold didn't bother me much. I had up lots of circulation.

Soon I heard Button heading uphill on the other side of Mineral Creek. That was a long ways from me, but it was a still day and I could hear him plainly. I wasn't having so much trouble following the trail now, and hurried along, listening as I went.

Then I heard Button jump the lion, and he sure did talk to her. She seemed to be heading for a place called Cooney Peak where there are lots of bad bluffs. It's a good place for a lion to get away. My hopes fell. But then the barking started coming toward me.

I like to think Button headed the cat away from those bluffs, but probably he didn't. I imagine she just got excited and happend to head my way.

As I was scrambling down, I heard Button barking treed near the bottom of the creek. I landed at the bottom of a dark little canyon with some big spruce trees in it. I doubt the sun ever hit in there in midwinter. I had to keep holding on to things to get around.

Then I saw the lion. She wasn't much more than 12 feet off the ground, on a big, dead spruce that had fallen and lodged in some other trees. The dead tree was lying just about level.

She was one of the prettiest lions I've ever seen. The tips of her ears, nose, and tail were jet black. She had a white belly, and her back was a light chocolate color.

I got out my old pistol and swung the cylinder to one side, held it up, and blew the snow and water out of the barrel. I spun the cylinder to see if it worked, then snapped it back in place. The cat began to switch the end of her tail in quick little jerks. In lion language, that meant she was going to do something.

I knew I'd better hurry and shoot. I used a little pine tree for a rest, aimed at her head, and fired, she never blinked an eye, just lashed her tail another jerk or two. I had to do something quick, so I emptied the gun, pointing it right at her middle without aiming it much.

I knew I hit her a time or two, because I saw her flinch, but she ran right up that log toward the mountainside and jumped off as if she weren't even hurt. Old Button sailed after her.

She hadn't gone far before he overtook her, and she went up another tree. I started climbing to get on the high side of her, knowing I'd get a lot closer that way. When I got up even with her, holding onto trees and jabbing my feet into the snow sideways, I still couldn't tell whether she was hurt.

I thought I'd get her right this time, so I took good aim at her shoulder and fired. She didn't move for a moment, then ran a little higher up the tree. I could tell now that I'd hit her. She turned and ran down the tree and on down the hill, Button on her heels.

It wasn't long before I heard Button barking treed. When I caught up with them, I saw a little blood dripping from one of the cat's legs. It seemed to me, the way she was holding it, that it was broken. She was badly hurt, and doing a lot of snarling and spitting.

I took aim and started shooting, and suddenly she came right down that limb toward me. I suppose all she wanted was to get away, but I wasn't taking any chances. I tried to run, but I just fell down and got up again about three times right in the same place.

The lion fell off the limb three or four feet away from me, but the hill was so steep she went end-over-end down the mountain like a ball rolling. Button kept after her. Soon I heard him barking and baying below me, and now I guessed the lion couldn't climb any more.

I was taking my time getting to her, holding onto trees and bushes, when all at once Button began to holler as if he was hurt. I knew the cat had a grip on him, and I sure was surprised for I thought he was too smart for that.

Now I threw caution to the winds, and slid down that hill lickety-split on my fanny. By the time I got near them I'd picked up so much momentum I couldn't stop. The cat was hanging onto some rock with her claws to keep from rolling down the hill, and Buttom was loose and standing back snappin and barking right into her face.

I tried desperately to grab something, but there wasn't any way I could stop sliding down toward that lion. All I could do was jump over her. So I did, and as I passed her I shot her right in the ear. I slid several more feet before I stopped, then made my way back up to see what had happend. She was dead all right.

I was cold, and it was so dark and wet in the canyon, that I thought first I might scalp her. But I don't like to scalp a lion. I think a lion should be skinned and the hide taken care of.

Before getting to work, I tried to make a fire. Usually I carry a candle and a little piece of inner-tube or some pitch, but this time I had only a couple of matches rolled up in a piece of bread paper. I picked up a spruce knot and beat it over a rock to loosen it up. Next to pine, this is about as good as anything. But when I lit it, I got such a small glow that I gave up the idea of making a fire.

I started in to skin the cat, and when I got right down over her and opened her up I found quite a bit of heat from her body. I decided not to skin out her claws to make the job go faster. Then to my surprise, I found that the last bullet I shot as I jumped over her was just stuck in her ear; it never even went through the hide. And of the previous shots, two or three bullets were lodged just barely under her skin. Some of my ammunition had been faulty. It had been even worse than my aim.

After I got home, I went behind the house and set up a one-inch board in front of a pine stump and took several shots at it with the .32/20. Some bullets went right through the board and into the stump, but others wouldn't even stick in the board. They just fell to the ground in front of it.

What happened was that I'd had two boxes of shells and had poured both of them into a little canvas bag before going on the hunt. Evidently one box was no good, but there was no way to tell the good from the bad. After that, I threw them all away.

After I got the cat skinned out I started around the south slope of the mountain where I'd left my jeep. Before I got there, the two other dogs, Slobber and Bob, overtook me. They'd run the back trail, given up, then had come the right way. They had been past the kill, and thought they were pretty smart, but they hadn't anything to do with catching that lion. Old Button did it all by himself.

Button had been bitten through a foot and in the fleshy upper part of a front leg. He bled quite a bit, but before we got out it had stopped.

After we got back to the jeep we were close to Willow Creek Ranch, so I went there to warm up and get a bite to eat. Len Shellhorn was there, and he made me a big hot toddy and gave me some stew. When I left him I felt like a different man.

Old Button knew he was suppose to be allowed in the house for special attention when he'd caught anything or done anything unusual. So when we got home he walked right up to the door and scratched at it with his good leg. My wife let him in and said. "Oh, so you caught something."

Well, that was the last trip anybody made over that road until the following spring. Len Shellhorn came out on horseback the next day. The wind blew some and another storm came up. The snow became too deep to navigate then, so all that wonderful back country got another long rest. The End.

NO DEFENSE

A TRUE TALE by T.J. (Shorty) Lyon,
Mogollon, New Mexico.

Illustrations by Herb Mott

Lion hunting in New Mexico, I got off my horse to follow
some tracks. Not expecting to go far, I left my rifle in the
saddle scabbard. I was unarmed.

I followed the tracks to a crack in the high bluff, and went inside it.

Stepping around a bend,
I saw a huge lion crouched on a narrow rock ledge.

Its tail switched ominously.
I knew it wanted out, and
I was in the way.

I tried to dislodge a rock or
stick to defend myself with,
but couldn't.

As the lion jumped, I hit the ground,
putting my head down
and covering up.

I felt a hard shove as the lion shot by, sending me sprawling in the dirt.

Since the, when hunting lions, I've always carried a hand-gun—just in case.

Illustrated by Herb Mot

Thin out the Negrito Creek lions, the boss ordered. Some came hard, like the big old grandpappy that Billy wounded.

A MONTH OF LIONS

I'd just finished up a job that I didn't like the least bit. I'd been helping Frank Lamb, predatory-control man for the U.S. Fish and Wildlife Service, put out 1080 poison. One thing for sure, you don't use any dogs on this job, and me being a hound-dog man I just naturally didn't like this work. But on January 1 we finished up.

The deer hunters and ranchers on Negrito Creek had been reporting an unusual number of lions and sign, such as deer kills and tracks. One party had seen four lions in a bunch and had killed one and thought they'd wounded another. Two other lions had been killed by deer hunters in nearby areas during the past deer season.

So Louis H. Laney, head of the Fish and Wildlife Service in New Mexico and my boss, said, "Shorty, maybe you better get your dogs and start at Earl Gilson's ranch at the head of the Negrito Creek and see if you can't thin the lions down some there. We've been getting too many reports on them in that area."

Nothing could have pleased me more. I felt like I'd just been let out of jail, and figured I'd take about a month up there.

Earl and Nina Gilson have a ranch up that way and are good friends of mine and very nice people. Earl is a ex-bear hunter, and for several years he had the best pack of bear dogs in this part of the country. I've known him to catch as many as 10 and 15 bears in a single season when he was in the business. He gave me old Slobber, my top dog before he died, when he was just a puppy. Earl is a hound-dog man at heart and we talk the same language.

When I told him I'd been assigned to hunt his country and that I'd like to camp at his place, he said there'd be no camping, that I'd stay with them and he'd hunt some with me. Well, I don't know what could have been better since I knew what a swell cook Nina was and all. Earl told me I needn't bring my saddle mule, Lupie, as he had several horses he was grain-feeding and I could ride one of those.

But just a few days before I was to leave, we had a snowstorm. We didn't get but six inches at Mogollon, the abandoned mining town in southwestern New Mexico that I call home, but I saw Earl at nearby Glenwood and he said there was 15 inches at the ranch. Now Earl also is our country commissioner, so he had a grader to clear the roads and we went in behind it. In the summer when the roads are open, it's only 28 miles from my place at Mogollon to Earl's ranch on the head of Negrito Creek, but when it snows it's something else. The road I had to take now as 145 miles instead of 28.

Negrito Creek is about 30 miles long, with picturesque country at its head. There are large open grass hills and meadows dotted with pines, but as you go down it becomes more rugged with lots of high bluffs and big canyons. About halfway down it crosses the boundary line of the Gila and Apache National Forests, and it runs into the San Francisco River just a short way below Reserve, New Mexico. To the north is Eagle Peak, which is a U.S. Forest Service lookout point that's about 10,000 feet high and covered with snow in winter. Bear Wallow, a lookout point to the south, also is about 10,000 feet.

After so much rest with no hunting, my dogs were pretty wild and hard to control. I'd been having trouble with them anyway since old Slobber had died. He was the daddy of three of my dogs and the grandfather of one. I had to keep the young dogs necked most of the time, but I used Minnie Bell, their mother, and Leavins, one of the oldest males, as strike dogs after we'd gone awhile and got the keen edge off them.

Earl and I hunted together on his range for a few days without finding any fresh sign. Then he and Nina went to Albuquerque, leaving me by myself, and that same day, hunting on one of Earl's horses, I found lion sign at a place called N Bar Park, where there's a big open flat dotted with pine trees. A lot of the country is jackpine thickets.

The snow was deep in most places. I showed the lion's track to the dogs, but they didn't pay any attention for it was too old for them to smell. We followed the track about a quarter of a mile and came to where the lion started to follow a porcupine trail.

This made things a little more interesting, but the dogs still couldn't smell anything. We didn't follow the procupine trail but a short ways until we come to where the lion had caught it. She (I suspected she was a female from her tracks) had made one long jump of about 20 feet. The snow was wallowed down a little, and there were a few quills and a large spot of blood. She picked it up and carried it about 100 yards to a large pine tree and there she'd eaten it, leaving the skin whole with the needles in it. I've often found where a lion has done this and hope someday to see it happen.

After eating the porcupine she went to another tree and slept, and now the dogs could smell her a little. I turned Minnie Bell lose first. She circled but couldn't seem to get anywhere, so I turned Leavins loose too. They all seemed so interested in the lion scent I got overconfident and turned them all loose. The only place they could smell her good enough to open on was where she'd slept. So they made bigger and bigger casts looking for more sign, and finally they ran plumb off until I couldn't hear them at all.

I sure felt disgusted. With so much snow it looked like anyone should find that lion's tracks. I made wider and wider circles looking but still couldn't find any. I decided she must be in a tree, so I looked in about 1,000 trees, but no lion did I see. I came to where she'd slept and stood there for several minutes trying to figure out what had happened.

It was about 25 feet from where I stood to the closest tree. The snow had melted off and left the dry pine needles under the trees, but there was better than a foot of snow everywhere else. By this time there were dog's tracks everywhere, which confused me more. The snow would fall down into these tracks and it was impossible to tell if they'd been made by the lion or the dogs.

I went from one tree to another, looking under them, and at the fourth tree I found a lion track in the edge of the snow. This lion was jumping and landing in the melted-out spots under the trees. Why she did it I don't know. Of course, if the trail had been fresh enough this wouldn't have helped her any, as the dogs would have trailed her anyway. It sure did fool me for awhile, but I knew what the score was now and made good time trailing her, even without the dogs.

Where the trees were too far apart for the lion to make it in one jump, she'd take 20 and 30-foot jumps, landing in the snow with all four feet together so that you couldn't see a plain foot-print. But that didn't matter now because I knew it was her sign and kept right on after her. After about a quarter of a mile I came to a large canyon. On my side there was solid snow so she'd quit jumping and walked slowly along, leaving a plain trail.

How I wished for my dogs, and I was very disgusted too for taking so long to figure out this lion. If I'd taken the dogs to this point sooner, I'd never have lost them.

Well, I knew I had to have them to catch this lion, so I rode back the way I'd come, calling for them. After about two miles I heard my little red-and-white spotted puppy, Skipper, howling. Skipper isn't but four months old and this was some of his first hunting. He'd gotten lost from the other dogs and was howling the way puppies do. I rode to him, and to my surprise, Junior, my young red dog, who's 1½ years old, was with him. I tried to find more dogs but couldn't, so I returned to where the lion had started into the canyon and put Junior on the trail.

We followed the trail to the bottom of the canyon, but on the other side there were dry patches of pine needles and we lost it. Once Junior got all excited and I thought we had a hot trail, but it turned out to be a bobcat track and we soon lost it too.

By now it had started to get dark, so I started back to the ranch feeling pretty disgusted. On my way in I heard a dog baying and I called, and Minnie Bell came. She's my oldest black-and-tan dog, age 3½ years, and has helped tree 35 or 40 lions. I felt better now because I knew with Minnie Bell I had a good chance to get Old Lady Longtail the next day.

As I said, I suspected this lion was a female, because her track was not too big and a little neater than a male's, and also because I hadn't found any scrapes. If it had been a male lion it most likely would have made some scrapes in the pine needles after eating and sleeping.

I was up early the next morning in 10-below temperature, which is extremely cold weather for this country, though the sun sometimes gets up warm enough later that it melts some of the snow.

I'd hoped that the other two dogs, Leavins and Zipper, would come in during the night, but they hadn't shown up. These two black-and-tans are 2½ years old, are well trained, and have been in on several lion kills. Minnie Bell is their mother and old Slobber was their father. They're really good dogs but just hadn't gotten enough hunting lately to settle them down. I sure wished for them this morning, but I still felt I could get that lion with the dogs I had if I got anything like a good trail.

So I took Minnie Bell, Junior, and Skipper, and headed back for N Bar Park. I picked up the old tracks and was following them into the canyon when the dogs all quit me and ran up the canyon side. They opened up with plenty of hound talk. I rushed after them, but Minnie Bell and Junior were on their way, making that canyon ring with hound music.

I went to where they'd made their start, hoping they were after the right thing. There was a fresh lion kill, so fresh it was still warm. The pup, Skipper, was helping himself to it. He seemed to prefer good hot venison to a hot lion trail.

I started after the dogs, but the canyon side was steep and there was lots of down timber so I wasn't moving very fast. Before I got to the bottom I heard them coming back, so I stopped and waited. I didn't wait long. They made a complete circle around me and then headed up the canyon. I rode after them as fast as I could.

After a short ways the canyon forked, I didn't know for sure which fork they'd taken so I went up the ridge between the two forks. I'd just topped out when I heard them coming back toward me in the canyon to my right. I pulled up and waited and they ran the lion right straight to me. They weren't 100 yards from me when I heard a scraping on the bark of a spruce tree as she hit it going up.

Old Minnie started barking treed right off, but Junior was circling around when I got there. Of course, as soon as I got off and started looking up he saw her and went to barking treed also.

She sure was pretty up there with her hind feet on one limb and her front feet about two feet higher up on another. She was looking down at us with her sides going in and out fast. As full of deer as she was, she'd given us a hard run.

I let the dogs bark at her for several minutes, and wished that Skipper was there too, but I guess he was still eating off her kill. I took a rest on a small pine tree and when she looked straight at me I put the sight of my .22 Remington Special half an inch above her eyes and touched it off.

She never knew what hit her. She struck the ground head first and was making hard kicks with her hind legs as she died. Junior kept running into her and getting kicked back until I was afraid he'd get cut by her claws, but he never did. He got a hold and began to bite and wool her in the flank, and Old Minnie had her by the back of the neck.

I started to walk around them and almost tripped over Skipper. I guess the barking and shooting was just more then he could stand, so he'd left his feast and joined us. He looked pretty full. When I gutted the lion and fed Minnie Bell and Junior the heart, liver, lungs, and kidney, Skipper wouldn't eat any. But when I opened up her stomach, which was full of deer meat, he sure went after that.

I loaded the lion in front of me on Old Tony, one of Earl's good horses, and he didn't do anything more than snort a little. I expected Earl had packed both lion and bear on him before.

I made a big circle looking for my other two dogs. I didn't find them, but I did cut their sign several places where they'd been back-trailing the lion we'd just caught.

The next day, I went by horseback to N Bar Park and found my dogs at the lion's kill. Old Leavins looked like a pumped-up balloon, he was so full of deer meat, and Zipper was starving. Leavins had his bluff in on Zipper, and he wasn't letting him have a bit to eat. That's brotherly love for you.

I had covered this country well by the time I'd found my dogs, so I decided to head down Negrito Creek. I'd gone so far from the Gilson ranch by mid-afternoon I was debating whether to go back or to ride on down to Billy Kiehne's, which now was much closer.

Billy is the son of Max Kiehne, who owns a large ranch here on Negrito Creek. Billy runs the ranch for his dad, and he also has a pack of lion and bear dogs. He's hound-dog minded too, same as Earl, so I always enjoyed a visit with him.

Then a big bobcat made up my mind for me. We started trailing him and he headed almost straight for the Kiehne Ranch. Just before dark we jumped him at the head of a little canyon where he'd just killed a young turkey gobbler. The dogs put him up in nothing flat and we ended his turkey eating right there. I carried him on down to Billy's, skinned him out there, and fed him to the dogs for supper.

I visited with Billy and his family for awhile, and Billy and I hunted with no luck. Then I returned to Mogollon for Lupie, my saddle mule, and came back and hunted with some old hunting partners who'd come visiting to Billy's ranch, and we did some lion business. After that I made camp about five miles below Billy's and Billy found time to hunt with me again.

I'd found the tracks of two lions three days before and had been hunting hard trying to find them. Billy suggested that we try Russ Ridge, a high rough ridge that runs for about 15 miles from Eagle Peak on the north to Apache Peak, on the south. It's a natural run for the big cats, so it stood to reason we might pick up the trail there.

But things didn't turn out that way. We started at Negrito Creek and hunted south toward Apache Peak. We traveled about eight miles of rough country that morning without picking up any good trails, although we did find one kill made by a lion. But it was too old to do us any good.

Now, when a lion hunter mentions finding a kill, he means the remains of a deer that a lion has killed, unless he says it's some other animal. That's because deer are the lion's chief source of food.

This particular kill was four-point blacktail buck, and it was all eaten up except the large leg bones and skull. Lions usually take good care of their kill, carrying it to a shady, cool place. and after eating their fill, covering it with pine needles or whatever other light material is handy so that it will keep in good shape. If they don't make a new kill they'll return and eat from it again. Sometimes a lion will bed down near its kill and eat from it until it's all gone, without making any attempt at a fresh kill.

We also found a coyote kill. Coyotes are quite different in their eating habits. These mountain coyotes usually run two or three in a small pack. They relay deer and run them down, then eat the entrails first and scatter the rest all over the country. They're pretty sure to return to their kills too, and it's a excellent place to trap them. But they make no pretense at saving or preserving anything.

There had been some coyotes at this kill recently, and Billy and I had to watch our dogs and keep scolding them so they wouldn't take the coyote trail. When lion dogs run coyotes it spoils them for treeing cats. Although coyotes can be caught with dogs in certain types of country, it's next to impossible to catch one here in these Rocky Mountains with dogs. So us cat hunters try to keep our dogs from having anything to do with them. However, we sometimes fail in doing this.

We had lunch and rested at a little open meadow on the west side of the Kiehne Ranch where there's a cow camp. The cow men sometimes work cattle there in the summer. It's called Sheep Basin. Although there are no sheep within miles. This is strictly cow country.

We unsaddled our mounts and let them roll, rest, and eat grass. The dogs stretched out in the warm sun and went to sleep. I had some fresh pork chops in aluminum foil and cooked them in our small fire for about 20 minutes. When we unwrapped them, they were a hot, tasty lunch.

Coming back in the evening, we started down a well-marked ridge and noticed quite a lot of lion sign like old droppings and scrapes made in the pine needles. When a male lion is traveling a regular run such as this ridge he scrapes in the direction he's going. The freshest scrapes we noticed, were going our way, although this sign was too old for the dogs to trail. But they knew it was lion sign, and kept testing it.

After three miles of going down this ridge, we turned down a steep hillside into a large canyon, and we'd just about reached the bottom when one of Billy's dogs, Old Sissy, opened up. Of course, all the dogs ran to her, as hounds always do.

I loped my saddle mule, Lupie, back up the ridge to try to get ahead of the dogs so that I could look for tracks, but before I'd gone very far the dogs all turned back and were barking around a log where Sissy had first opened up.

On my way back I saw a fresh coyote track in a patch of snow and my heart sank, because I thought they were trying to start a coyote trail. My young red dog, Junior, sure does love to run a coyote, and I saw he was especially interested in this scent. So I jumped off my mule and got after him and made him stop trailing. I also hollered to Billy to get his dogs off the scent, and he did.

Then I heard my oldest dog, Minnie Bell, open up just around the hillside and I rushed to stop her. But to my surprise, she was standing over a very fresh lion scrape under a large juniper tree. This sure put a different light on the whole deal.

I called to Billy and he rushed over with his dogs. When his old dog, Sissy, got a good smell of that scrape she just pointed her nose up to the sky and sounded in a way that made an old hound-dog man's heart rejoice. She said in good old plain hound language, "This is it, this is lion, and no mistake about it. It's fresh enough, it's good. All you young dogs gather round, we got work to do."

Now of course if a man didn't savvy hound-dog language, he couldn't have understood all that Old Sissy was saying. But Billy and me, we savvied mucho. We're the breed.

I'm telling you, from there on business picked up. We had eight dogs with us and those eight dogs set out to catch them a lion. They crossed the canyon quick, but up on the other side they slowed when they had to work to find the trail. But man oh man, how they did work. It was slow, but they never did completely lose the scent, and every dog was working his very best. There was music there in them mountains that should have been recorded.

All this time I was having trouble getting my mule up the

steep icy slope after the dogs. It was slick, and danger from falling was considerable. In fact, Billy's horse did take a bad fall, but didn't get seriously hurt.

When we finally topped out, we couldn't hear the dogs because they'd outdistanced us. This is the most depressing thing that can happen to a lion hunter, when he knows his dogs are going to tree a lion and maybe he won't be able to find them. The only thing left for us to do was to hunt and listen for them.

Billy took the east side of the ridge and I the west, and we started riding. We'd only gone a short distance when I heard them off below in the same canyon that we'd just come out of. I called to Billy, since the dogs were on my side and he couldn't hear them.

As soon as Billy topped the ridge on my side and could hear the dogs, he said, "Old Sissy's barking treed," and then I too heard them barking treed. We wasted no time getting off to them.

There he was, Mr. Gentleman Longtail, and a big old grandpappy at that, high up in a big pine tree, looking down on eight barking dogs, two men, a horse, and a mule. I bet he thought that was quite a gathering.

Well, Billy had his .30/30 Winchester out and was looking like he wanted to do the shooting, so I said to him, "Billy, are you a good shot?"

He replied, "I reckon I'm good enough, but just what do you mean?"

I said, "What I mean is, that shore is a big lion, and I want him dead when he hits the ground so he won't hurt any of the dogs."

Billy said he thought he could kill him O.K., so I said, "all right, let him have it," and he took aim and fired.

He had a gun he hadn't shot very many times, and I guess he was a little excited. I don't know of anyone that wouldn't be some excited, looking up at that big cat. I know my heart was sure pounding.

Anyway, he just wounded him in the shoulder and side, and that big old fellow sure clawed and fought to hang onto that limb he was on, but after two or three attempts he half fell and half jumped out of the tree. He jumped enough to clear the dogs and took off around the hillside. He actually outran the whole pack of dogs for about 500 yards, wounded as he was and trailing blood, but they overtook him in a little canyon.

About the most dangerous thing that can happen is to get a large wounded lion at bay on the ground, and I think the only thing that saved us from losing some dogs was the fact that we had so many dogs they just overpowered him. All eight of our dogs took to him at the same time. I don't think that there was a one that hesitated about going in and getting a hold, even to the youngest dog in the pack. But we didn't get off scot-free by any means.

The minute I saw what had happened I ran for my mule and took after them. For a short ways the going was down a steep, icy hillside, and although I was kicking my mule, Lupie, and jobbing her with my rifle butt, I could not get her to run. She had more sense than me, and knew it was too dangerous to run down that frozen hillside. That's one good thing about a mule, they're cool-headed no matter what.

By this time the dogs had caught the lion, and he was down on his back in a small wash fighting them off. Cats often will lie on their backs while fighting dogs. This gives them a chance to use all four clawing feet, as well as their teeth.

I could hear one dog yelling for help above the other voices, and I knew I had to get to him quick or I'd have a dead dog. So I jumped off my mule, who was taking short, careful steps on the ice, and off I went, half-running and half-sliding down the hillside.

I could see that the lion had a claw hung onto a leg of one of my big young dogs and was trying to pull him down to his mouth to finish him off.

There was no time for fooling around. I had to get in close enough to put my .22 Remington Special against the lion's head so that I wouldn't hit any of the dogs. This I did, and pulled the trigger and killed the lion. But I still had to take the lion's foot and move him and my dog, Zipper, around to where I could get the huge claw out of Zipper's leg. The lion had also bit poor old Zipper through both front feet, which crippled him considerably. But as far as I could tell, there were no broken bones.

Billy had come sliding off the hill right behind me, and now he felt awful bad about wounding the lion and was trying to apologize. I told him to forget it, that I'd done much worst things myself, and I was thankful that we didn't get any dogs killed.

Another dog of mine, Junior, was bit through the ear, and the way his ear was folded at the time it made three holes it in, but it wasn't anything serious. Billy's old dog, Sissy, had a bad limp when she walked, but the skin wasn't broken anywhere. I think probably the lion gave her a hard cuff and sprang her shoulder. Everyone was happy exept Zipper, Junior, and Sissy, but I was sure they were going to be O.K. The End.

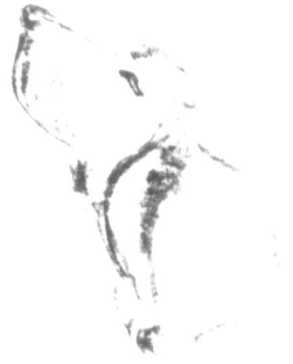

Trusted Friend

It's
true what
they say about
a dog being man's best friend, some of mine I called:

"A good dog is
as essential to
the hunter as a
horse is to
a cowboy."

(Old) Button
(Old) Slobber
(Old) Minnie Bell
Squeaker
Eckebod
Blue Boy

(Old) is a earned title added with age and respect by the master.

Illustrated by John McDermott

When I squeezed off a blast, the big cat came boiling out of the brush, both front feet pawing at his head.

LION WASN'T MY AIM

The big lion was going up the steep hillside in long, easy leaps. The hill was much too steep for my saddle mule to make any time, and the big cat was already out of range of the shotgun I was carrying. I was at a loss as to what I should do for a moment, and then I thought of my newly purchased varmint call. I pulled my mule, Old Lupie, to a stop, got out the call, and blew a loud blast that sounded to me like a dying calf in a hailstorm.

I think the sound reached the lion while he was in mid-air, and when he hit the ground he came to a dead stop. He just stood there and listened for about a minute. Then he began to fidget around some, so I let go with the call again. This time I really "got with it," as Bear Turner says. I blew it high and shrill, low and mournful, and everything I could think of in between

When I finally stopped for breath, that lion never hesitated. He came right back over his tracks and straight for me in a long, fast trot. I could hardly believe my eyes.

I was riding out from Willow Creek on October 25th to patrol the north end of the Gila Wilderness Area during the 1959 special deer, turkey, and bear season. New Mexico's Department of Game and Fish allows its conservation officers to take legal game while on duty so long as they don't let it interfere with doing a good job for the department.

I didn't much want a bear, and I'd already spoiled my deer

hunting by killing a nice, big, mule deer buck a few days earlier. So now what I was mostly interested in was a fat turkey gobbler for the coming Thanksgiving. That's why I was carrying the old, "Long Tom" Iver Johnson 12 guage. It has put a few gobblers on the table before, and I was hoping it would do so again. I knew I wasn't going to shoot a bear with it, and I never dreamed of seeing a lion without my dogs (no dogs are allowed in these special hunting areas).

I have hunted lions and lived in lion country better than 30 years, and up to this time I had seen only one lion without the help of traps or dogs. So I wasn't lion hunting. I was patrolling and hoping to get a shot at a turkey.

I had never owned a game call until just a few days earlier. It seems like I keep putting off the best things in life, such as tying flies, loading shells, taking pictures, and blowing varmint calls. I read and hear about how much fun everyone else is having doing these things, and I aim to start doing them myself in just a short time, but I just keep putting them off. I had been thinking of getting a call for about 10 years. Now that I have one, I realize what I've been missing.

Bear Turner, who lives in Magdalena and is a district conservation officer for the Department of Game and Fish, is also a blower of the calls. Three days previously, Bear and I sat on our mules on top of a little hill overlooking a beautiful mountain glade with Bear instructed me in the finer art of blowing the call. I had given mine a half-hearted blow or two when Bear said, "Shorty, you don't just toot around a little. What you've got to do is really get with it."

So he proceeded to show me. Believe me, he made that innocent-looking little whistle sound like something caught between hellfire and brimstone. It made my hair stand on end and goose pimples rise all over me. I soon had both ears and a head full of it and was just fixing to tell him I'd had enough when I saw a movement on the other side of the park.

Next thing I knew, two coyotes were more than halfway across and coming at a dead run. "Get your gun, here they come," I hollered.

We both jumped off our mules so fast we frightened them and the coyotes too. By the time we got our guns out, there wasn't anything to shoot at.

"Bear, did you ever see a couple of chumps likes us before?" I asked.

Bear laughed, "Yea, we sure goofed," he said. "But don't worry you can always call up some more."

Well, a turkey was still No. 1 on my list, so when I found a likely looking spot I'd first use my turkey call. I knew a heap more about what I was doing with it, but if I couldn't get any response from the gobbler call, I'd let go with the varmint one hoping to call up a fox, bobcat, or coyote.

Sometimes I felt plumb ashamed of myself for breaking the peaceful solitude of the beautiful mountain parks with that gosh-awful, screaming, shrieking, howling noise that was suppose to sound like a rabbit or a fawn in agony or distress. Believe me, it's sure hard to describe what one of these calls does sound like. It makes a racket like some baby animal or human in its last agonies. I've heard small babies having trantrums that sounded a lot like some of the noises it makes. I have also heard little fawns that an eagle had caught, and rabbits hung on a wire fence that made similar sounds that you just have to imagine, but whatever sound it makes, it works.

It's true that I hadn't been able to call up anything I wanted to kill since the coyotes that Turner and I had goofed on, but I'd been doing a lot of practicing. I had called up quite a variety of birds, squirrels, chipmunks, and a few does. I had begun to think that perhaps I was learning something about the art of blowing a call.

I was some surprise, though, when I saw this big lion coming straight for me. About half the time I could see him as he trotted in my direction, but a part of the time he was hidden from sight by the low brush.

To tell the truth, I was not really sure I wanted to be such an excellent caller after all. However, I knew if I let him get close enough I could take care of him all right with the shotgun, so I pulled the hammer back before he got halfway to me. When he did get about halfway, which was still much too far for the old 12 guage, he suddenly stopped and sat down in a little clearing.

I let him sit for a few minutes. I was trying to figure it all out.

At first I'd supposed he knew what Lupie and I were, but now I begun to wonder. There was some thin gambel oak that had shed its leaves screening us just as little. At first I'd been on the mule. Then later I was standing close to her, so I reasoned that perhaps the lion didn't know for sure there were two of us and that I was a man.

With this thought in mind, I stayed close to Lupie and tied her to a small oak. Then I dropped down in the trail on my stomach and started slowly crawling and pulling myself along with my elbows. I had in mind to crawl to a log about 50 yards down the trail which would put me straight under the lion and perhaps close enough for a shot.

I could see the lion through the dead ferns and grass which was about 18 inches high along the trail. I'd crawled but a few feet when the lion stood up and looked back up the hill as if perhaps he was thinking about quitting me. So I got my caller out and began a low, mournful wailing. This seemed to satisfy him, and he settled down on his haunches again and continued to look in my direction.

I pulled myself along with my elbows, making very slow progress, and several times the lion got nervous. At these times I'd blow the call and he'd quiet down. Twice he answered me with a peculiar, birdlike whistle — something few people ever have the privilege of hearing. It is most likely to be heard when young kittens have been taken away from their mother. Then they occasionally make the whistling sound, but it's a very rare thing to hear. Also, I was sure that this was a large, mature, male lion.

I felt a little scared. I was afraid there might be two lions, and maybe one of them wouldn't know I was a man.

I tried to look in all directions, but the willows on my right came up within a few feet of me and were so dense I couldn't see more than a foot or two into them.

Besides being somewhat scared, I felt pretty silly. I reminded myself of a character in a movie I saw a few years ago. This miserable, deformed, and twisted wretch pulled himself along on the ground inches at a time until he came to the feet of a healer who cured him with supernatural powers. It was a scene from a film about the career of Lon Chaney. I'm sure anyone who saw this picture will appreciate the comparison.

Of course, if I'd been standing up on my feet in a man's manner I would have had nothing to fear from a mountain lion, but I wasn't doing this. Instead, I was a crawling, mourning, crippled creature no more than a foot high. I half expected the lion to charge me from the hillside any second. I knew he could reach me in seconds, too. I also knew that I'd have to get in a different position before I could aim my gun. I would have to get to my knees at least. Though a little frightened, I don't think I was really nervous. I felt I had the situation under control, but this feeling didn't last long.

I had crawled down the trail toward two large pine trees that I had to pass. These trees were on the hillside between me and the lion, and I knew that I'd lose sight of him for a moment when I passed the trees. Naturally I speeded up some when I passed the first tree. Everything was O.K. He was still sitting there in plain sight looking down my way. I gave him a few mournful sounds on the call so he would still think I was badly hurt. I was still watching the lion mighty close.

When I came to the second pine tree, about 10 or 12 feet farther down the trail, I rested just a little, then made a fast crawl past it. When I looked to where I thought the lion should have been I didn't see him. At first I thought perhaps I hadn't gone far enough, and I made some real crawling time for a few feet more, never taking my eyes off the spot where I thought he ought to have been. Well, he wasn't there, and that's all there was to it.

Now I really had something to worry about. It was altogether a different matter when I could see him. Not knowing where he was, and having been trying to make him think I was a poor crippled, harmless thing for so long, made me afriad I had succeeded, and that he'd spring on me out of the brush.

For an instant I almost panicked. I wanted to stand up and sing him a little of The Battle of New Orleans so he'd be sure I was a man after all. But I wasn't quite scared enough for that. However, I made record time crawling to the log I'd been heading for, and I left off all the weird sounds that had been accompanying my crawl up to then.

There was some slight comfort in the big pine log. I could

get about half of me up hard and safe against it. Time sure began to drag, and I was wondering if Lupie and I were by ourselves or if we still had company.

I tried to look in all directions at the same time, and my neck was getting tired. There wasn't anything else to do, so I blew the call again, but I really didn't have my heart in it this time.

A few seconds passed, then the lion gave me a low whistle. It sounded close, but I couldn't tell for sure where it came from. If it had been possible to look any better than I'd already been doing, I would have done so, but I'd been looking my very best ever since he'd disappeared. One thing I knew, he was still with me.

Well, I stayed by that log for about two hours. That's not very long, it's true, if you're watching a good television show or leaning back in your favorite chair. But things were different there at the log.

All my life, I have heard water trickling over rocks and sticks as it makes its way toward the sea, but the little stream nearby made some of the strangest sounds I have ever heard. It made all kinds of noises, such as that of a large, house cat purring, or a body slipping through the willows, and lots of other sounds that you couldn't rightly describe. At times there was some distant thunder that I could barely hear. It started with sort of a growl, then became a rumble. Once a croaking sound started up on the ridge and worked clear around me into the willows where it finally completed its language into the caw of a crow. But when it did let me know what it was, it didn't help too much. I figured it was probably carrying on because the lion was close by.

If you think two hours isn't a long time, you should try two hours in the brush with an unseen lion.

I had all I wanted of it. I didn't sing any of The Battle of New Orleans, but I stood straight up, cleared my throat real loud, and spit. Nothing happened. I thought to myself that I was probably pretty foolish. Likely the lion was miles away by now.

Nevertheless, I was keeping a keen lookout as I walked back to my mule, and that's how I came to see the cat again. I could just barely make out his face, he blended so perfectly with the grass, brush, and rocks. It's a wonder I saw him at all.

He'd moved down a good bit closer, but it was still a mighty long shot for the old shotgun.

I know now that I did the wrong thing. I should have tried to get closer, but I also knew that he could just make one little move and I wouldn't be able to see him. Besides, I'd been under considerable strain for the past 2½ hours. It wasn't quite like I'd just walked out of church.

I judged it to be about 55 yards, and uphill. I knew it sure was going to strain the old, Long Tom with its No. 4 shot, but I was ready for some kind of action. I took careful aim, putting the little round front sight on an oak leaf about six inches over the face I could barely see. I thought perhaps I could blind him and then get close enough to get him with another shot.

I squeezed her off. Man, I wish you could have seen that lion boil up out of the brush. He went straight up so high that I could see a lot of clearance between his long tail and the bushes, and he was pawing at his head with both front feet. When he came down, he hit on all fours and disappeared in the brush down the hillside toward me and just a few feet from where he was when I shot him.

I tried to reload the old single barrel as quickly as I could, but the shell didn't eject completely, and there was a moment when I took my eyes off the hill to get the empty shell out. I'd been trying to get the fresh one in on top of it. I didn't think I'd glanced away long enough for the lion to go anywhere, so I supposed he was still there in the brush. But I didn't know exactly where he was or how badly he was hurt.

Things didn't seem to be getting any better. I really had got myself in a mess now. I stood and watched for a long, long time, but nothing moved. I finally had to do something, but I didn't just walk into the place where he'd been hit.

There was a rockslide about 40 yards below, and I started climbing up the middle of it. The slide was about 50 feet wide, so I had 25 feet on each side of me with no brush or grass. From the top of the rockslide, I worked my way over until I was just above where the lion had been. Then I started slowly working down to the place I'd last seen him. Let me add just one little detail here: I had the hammer back on that scattergun.

In places the scrub oak was about waist high, and there was

a lot of high grass and different kinds of rocks. Most of the rocks were gray with greenish moss on them, but there were also some brownish-tan ones that were the exact color of the lion. I kept seeing these through the brush, and once in a while little birds would startle me with their quick movements. But anyway I was getting some action. I don't think it was quite as bad as sitting and waiting by the log had been.

I worked slowly and thoroughly. After about 30 minutes with no wounded lion jumping on me, I began to feel normal again. I tried to find some blood or hair, but there were no tracks, hair, blood, or anything else. The cat had just evaporated.

The crow was making quite a fuss back on top of the ridge now. I figured the lion might have been the cause of his making such a racket, but I also thought he might have been carrying on because of a kill the lion might have made and, even then, be feeding on.

It had been a long time since I'd had breakfast and I was getting hungry. I picked a place where I could watch the hillside, unsaddled Lupie, staked her in some good wild oats, and made a little twig fire. Then I put on a tin can for tea, opened a can of hot tamales, and set them on the fire in the can. I soon had a good lunch, using a piece of aluminum foil for a plate. I sat down with my back to a tree where I could watch the hillside.

After eating, I rested for a while and thought things over. The crow was still doing a lot of squawking up on the ridge, so I decided to climb up there and see if I could find anything. I'd come to the conclusion that I really hadn't hurt the lion very badly.

I struck out carrying a trap that I'd been packing on the back of my saddle. About halfway up the slope there was a long opening through the brush that led up to some high cliffs, on my right. A large, old fir tree, dead and rotten, had fallen into a part of the cliff. There were many pieces of it scattered around among the rocks, and one of the pieces looked very much like a lion. It even had a long, black tail hanging down. But I thought the tail was too black for a lion and probably was a manzanita root.

About the time I'd thoroughly convinced myself it wasn't a lion, it got up and turned around a couple of times. Then it lay down again facing back down the slope where I had come from.

This was something, seeing the lion again after shooting him in the face. That old proverb, curiosity killed the cat, surely was working in that direction here.

I felt sure he hadn't seen me yet, but I knew I couldn't go straight to him without him seeing me. I could see a place about 20 yards above him in the cliffs from which I thought I might get another shot at him. It would take a lot of hard, careful climbing. I sure wished for a rifle, but that didn't help any. I'd been wishing for a rifle or for some of my dogs for the past four or five hours.

I've never made a stalk for a caribou or grizzly bear in the far north. Neither have I ever stalked big game in Africa or India, though I've often wished I had an opportunity to do so. Well, here was a chance to do some real stalking right in my own forest, so I set out to do it.

Some places I had to crawl to keep out of the lion's sight, but most of the time I could stand up. When I'd start a rock to rolling I'd cuss and pray at the same time. I cussed the rock for making a noice and prayed that the lion couldn't hear it.

The wind was blowing in gusts, sometimes one way and sometimes another. I was afraid it would carry my scent to the lion. Whenever it blew hard it helped to quiet the sound I was making, and at these times I'd climb fast until it started to slack up, then I would have to go slow again. I could see the lion once in a while, but most of the time I was in brush too thick to see through.

When I finally reached the cliff I'd picked out above him, I started to peep over it. I believed I'd made a good stalk, and I expected to see the lion in easy range when I looked over the rim of the cliff. But there was no lion there.

I wasn't too discouraged at first. There were 100 places near-by that he could have moved to and still be in range. But, as I continued to sit quitely and look over the cliffs below me, I began to realize that I'd come out second best. The lion just wasn't there. Somewhere along the way he'd got wise to me and left.

I went to the flat rock he'd been lying on and looked for

blood, but there wasn't a trace of it. I knew he had spent considerable time on this rock, so if he'd been badly hurt there would surely have been a little blood. If he was going to get away, I hoped he wasn't in bad shape.

I've skinned out a number of lions that have had several porcupine quills embedded in their faces. The wounds caused by the quills had healed up perfectly and I don't believe the few pellets my lion received did him too much harm. I've also skinned out bears, coyotes, and lions that had been carrying bullets for years. Apparently — if the animal isn't hit internally — nature forms a protective substance around such things.

I hunted among the cliffs until dark without ever finding a trace of the lion, then I had a long ride back to camp.

I was up early the next morning and rode Lupe at a fast trot back to the spot. This time I had my Model 70, scope-sighted .300 and some snares, but they did me no good. I didn't see the lion nor did I find any kill or see anyplace where I thought I could get him in snare or trap. To tell the truth, I am kind of glad I didn't.

I wanted to get that lion, of course, but he'd given me the most exciting afternoon of my hunting life. So if some hound-dog hunter should tree and shoot a lion and find a few no. 4 shots under his skin, let him know he wasn't the only one to get a thrill from that old black-tail cat. I was there first, and while I was I did some high-voltage living. The End.

Rugged bluffs the mountain lion favors. Old Minnie Bell in the foreground.

Illustrated by Tom Beecham

A SPOILED LION

There was a strong draft of air at the old mine entrance, and the first two matches I struck were blown out before I had a chance to see anything.

But the third match made a big fizzle and then burst into flame as I held it high over my head. I had time for only a brief glimpse before it too went out, but in that short second I saw more sheer excitement than most people see in a lifetime.

At my feet was a great gaping hole going straight down. Out in the middle of his hole, 10 to 12 feet from either side on a rotten 8x8 timber, crouched a very angry mountain lion. Her black-tipped ears lay back tight against her head, her tail lashed back and forth in quick short jerks, and her lips wrinkled up showing a full set of yellow fangs and teeth. One foot was raised high with its needle-sharp claws poised for a lightning-fast strike.

She was spitting and hissing in angry cat fashion, and mingled with her sounds and the frantic barking of my dog, Old Squeaker, was a sizzling that came from a four-foot rattlesnake coiled with head high on a narrow ledge no more than two feet from my dog.

But what scared me even more than the lion or the snake was the danger of Squeaker's falling off the timber. I knew that the old mine shaft was probably several hundred feet deep, and Squeaker was charging back and fourth on the timber and half falling off at every charge.

The lion, wise one that she was, knew that she had him at a disadvantage on the narrow timber, and she was just waiting for one quick slap that would send him spinning into the old shaft.

I work for the New Mexico Department of Game and Fish. My newest title is Conservationist. I have been called a lot of things — some not too complimentary - but what I really am is a trapper and a hound-dog hunter. I have worked at this interesting occupation most of my life. I believe that the best compliment I have ever received was to be called a self-made naturalist. I have very little formal education, but I believe I could rate a PhD in wildlife knowledge for the area I have worked in.

I have had a few other stories published in *Outdoor Life*. They were about exciting lion hunts in this area. But the experience I had with the lion in the old abandoned mine tops them all.

Among other things, I have a small cattle ranch here at my home in Mogollon (Mug-e-own), New Mexico. Mogollon was for years a prosperous little mining town producing gold and silver, but World War II and a lack of high-grade ore shut down the mines in 1942. So Mogollon had been a ghost town for the past 28 years.

My small ranch is made up of patented mining claims, which I lease. The country is mighty rough and consists of a lot of old abandoned mines, some of which were shut down before I came to Mogollon 33 years ago.

It also comes close to being the best lion country left in the United States. I, for one, am very thankful for this fact, since lion hunting with dogs is my favorite sport. During my 33 years here I have taken a lot of lions; I have also been on many hunts where I came out second-best.

Sometimes I have caught lions with incredible ease, but not often. Most lions will give a good account of themselves if they are not hampered by some disadvantage.

Here I would like to discuss what we lion hunters call a spoiled lion.

In any area where lions are plentiful, almost every mountain range will have at least one really smart lion that gives lion hunters plenty of headaches. And contrary to what might be expected, it will invariably be a little female, probably not weighing more than 75 pounds. She will be light on her feet and able to run like a coyote and stay ahead of pursuing hounds for hours. And she will know every crack and crevice in every high bluff where she can slip down and get away from the dogs. She usually is a calf-killer too. I can't explain why, because a lion of this sort wouldn't have any trouble killing deer.

I was very surprised once when my friend and fellow hound-dog hunter Blue Rice, who lives down on Sacaton Creek, asked me about trapping a lion of this kind on his range.

"Why don't you catch her with your dogs?" I asked.

Blue replied that she was too smart and too fast for him and his dogs.

Another famous local lion hunter, Roy Snyder, who for years hunted lions for the New Mexico Game and Fish Department, had a spoiled lion over in the Pueblo Creek county that was really a nuisance to him. Whenever his dogs struck her he always said: "Well we might as well try to catch the dogs and go in; that's the little old spoiled lion. I can tell by the way the dogs are running, and there's one thing I know for sure: we ain't about to catch her."

Once the famous Ben Lilly said: "I have a little old spoiled lion over on the Sapillo that I am going to have to trap if she don't stop killing baby calves."

Well, my Old Smarty was a real spoiled lion if ever there was one. She not only knew how to made a good pack of dogs look foolish, but she also was highly educated in the art of staying out of steel traps. For this lesson she had paid a price. When I first found her track she had two middle toes missing on her right front foot. This handicap, if it was one, sure didn't slow up her running. It might have bothered her some in climbing a tree, but I wouldn't know about that because I never got close enough to her to make her want to climb a tree.

One time a few years back, after I had run Old Smarty off and on for three or four years, I thought I had her for sure. A lion had been heading for a crack in a 400-foot bluff, where Old Smarty had got away from me before, when the dogs caught her on the ground. I could tell by the noise they were making that they were having one heck of a fight.

My mule Lupie and I weren't long in getting to the scene, but there wasn't much left for me to do. I had six big hounds with me that day, and they just about had the lion killed. I gave her a mercy shot, but she was a young lion with no toes missing.

In a way I was glad, for such an end wouldn't have been very fitting for Old Smarty. And besides, now I still had her to hunt. (Sometimes I think we lion hunters are a little touched in the head.)

I next struck Old Smarty three or four months later. She had killed one of my calves, and I got her trail hot right off the kill. I figured that since she was full, maybe I'd get her. It was wishful thinking.

About two inches of fresh snow was on the ground, and it should have helped. We had run Old Smarty straight west for about half a mile to Gold Hill, atop a high bluff, when I over-took the dogs. Old Minnie Bell, my top dog, gave me a funny look, and I knew we were in trouble.

I got off my mule and tried to help the dogs decipher the tracks. Now I discovered something new. A toe was now miss-ing from Old Smarty's left hind foot, and the wound was fresh enough to leave a faint trace of blood in the snow. She had pro-bably stepped into a blind set made for coyotes. I knew that by now she was too smart to get caught in a baited trap.

Well anyway, I thought this fairly fresh wound would give us a mighty good chance to get her. I discovered that she had backtracked on us, so I quickly got the dogs headed back the way we had come.

Old Smarty went back by the kill and, to my surprise, took time to stop and relieve herself. Now with an empty stomach, she was ready to show us a thing or two, even if she did have a few missing toes, including one that was still sore.

She headed for Cooney Canyon, a place of high bluffs and deep crevices. Here she went off the rim into a real rock jungle that made for slow trailing. By the time we got down and across the canyon and started up the other side, which had southern exposure, the snow had melted off and Old Smarty's tracks and scent had gone with it.

I ran her a dozen times or more in the next five or six years, and during that time I caught several other lions whose trails she had crossed while I was trying to catch her. Sometimes it seemed as if she were a kind of Judas who deliberately steered me into other lions, knowing she would get away.

So Old Smarty was getting quite old. She had outlived my top dog, Old Minnie Bell, and now at the head of my pack was one of Minnie's puppies, Squeaker.

It was last May when I drove to the back side of my ranch to check some feed troughs for my cattle. I had taken the day off from my official duties with the Game Department. I was not hunting, but Old Squeaker was with me.

At the last trough a little heifer with a big bag was doing a lot of bawling. This behavior might mean any of several things. Maybe her calf had fallen into some old assessment hole and could be rescued. Assessment holes are dug 10 feet deep when a claim is first made on a mine. As the years pass these holes gradually fill up so that they are not very deep.

But when I saw some crows fly up out of the head of a little canyon, my hopes fell. Crows are real tattletales. Whenever something happens, they are the first to know. And they never keep anything to themselves. They shout it to the world, and they are not very particular about what they fuss over. They will put on just as big a show over a newborn calf as they will over one that has been killed.

Old Squeaker was already halfway down the little canyon by the time I decided to go. He savvies crows. Before I made it down he had circled the kill, picked up a trail, and left in a dead run.

"Whatever he's after was laying up with the kill," I said to myself.

I got to the bottom, and the sign was easy to read. It was my calf, all right, and a lion had killed it. A telltale circle of fine needles with which the lion had covered the calf after eating her fill was raked up in a big round pile. But the calf was no longer covered by the needles. Some coyotes had found it and drug it out and down the canyon and then they had eaten nearly all of it.

I figured that Squeaker had taken after a coyote and that he would soon be back. About 30 minutes later he returned, panting and tired, and lay down to rest for a short while before he got up and went to work.

Fresh coyote tracks and droppings were all over the area, but Squeaker paid no attention to them now. He nosed all over the big pile of pine needles, then made slow, ever-widening circles. Finally he stopped out about 100 yards, pointed his head at the sky, and gave out with a long, lonesome, mournful bawl.

I tried to help him, but the ground was so hard that I couldn't see a track. We worked the area for about a mile over to the rim of Cooney Canyon, and there I picked up some tracks. We were going the wrong way. Squeaker had got the backtrack.

But I saw something else: some toes were missing from some of those tracks. We were after Old Smarty.

It was a good feeling to know she was still alive. It had been a long time since I had last struck her. I thought perhaps she had died and gone wherever lions go. I think that there are surely a few lions like Old Smarty up in dog heaven. Otherwise it wouldn't really be heaven for a good lion dog.

I had no trouble turning Old Squeaker around. As soon as I encouraged him to go the other way he threw up his head, bawled, and took off back to the kill without making a stop. When he got there he made a couple of circles and then picked up the trail going the other way.

The track led us back by my pickup. It was now getting quite dark, and I had left my flashlight back at the house, but the moon was coming up over Spring Mountain and I figured that if it got high enough I might be able to get the lion between me and the moon and shoot my scope rifle.

I had been carrying my little Remington .22 W.R.F. that has served me faithfully for 33 years. But I left it in the truck and picked up my old army-issue Winchester .30/06 with a Weaver 4X scope. This rifle has been sporterized and, though still pretty heavy compared with the .22, is more dependable for night shooting.

By the time I changed rifles, Squeaker was halfway down Johnson Canyon and really going strong. I took off after him, sliding and holding onto the brush.

The old Johnson Mine was at the bottom of the canyon, but I

never once thought Old Smarty would take refuge in a mine.

I was about halfway down when I began to hear Squeaker loud and clear. He was barking treed, and the sound echoed back and forth.

I came sliding down with a lot of loose rocks just above him and was almost to the bottom when his barking stopped. After reaching the bottom of the canyon I stopped and listened but could not hear a sound — a development that I thought was very strange. Then, after working my way slowly along for about 100 yards, I began to hear the muffled sounds of Squeaker and the lion coming out of the old Johnson Mine.

I had trouble locating the mine's entrance in the dark because it had become overgrown with scrub oak, but I finally found it and very carefully made my way inside until I was only a few feet from the melee. Then I stopped and tried to light a match so I could see what was going on. The third match lit up to reveal the startling scene that I described at the beginning.

I backed up a safe distance from the shaft and began pleading with Squeaker to come back. I whistled, sweet-talked, and cussed him, and after what seemed like a long time I felt him touch my leg. I grabbed him by the collar and backed out to the mine's entrance.

It was obvious that I couldn't do anything without a light, so with some misgivings about Squeaker's safety I tied him to a small oak bush at the entrance and started climbing up the canyon as fast as my 62 years and over-weight condition would permit.

I reached the truck and drove the three miles to my house as fast as the rough road would allow. I got my light and some other things I might need and then decided to take a couple of young dogs I was training. Eckebod and Blue Boy, back with me. My wife had gone to a Women's Club meeting at the Glenwood, so there was no one to help — or to interfere — with my plans.

When I reached the canyon rim I necked up the young dogs and made them stay behind me. I couldn't hear Squeaker barking but didn't worry much about it. There was a very small chance that the lion might come out and attack him, but I was more concerned about his getting loose and falling down the mine shaft.

By the time I was halfway down the canyon wall Squeaker started baying. The sound got stronger and stronger, and the two young dogs started giving me trouble. They knew what he was saying, and they wanted to get in on the action. When we were just a few hundred yards from the mine, they got away from me. Now I was afraid that the two dogs, being necked together the way they were, would knock each other into the shaft.

When I rushed into the mine past Old Squeaker, sure Eckebod had fallen over the edge of the shaft. He was trying to get back out, and Blue Boy was sitting back with all his might trying to keep from going in too. I got hold of them and pulled them out past Squeaker and tied them with a chain I had brought. I put another chain on Squeaker to make him safer, so now I had the dogs under control.

As I approached the shaft with a good light, all three dogs were barking so that it was almost impossible to hear anything else. The mine magnified the sound until it was just a continuous roar. But since I was already spooked on the rattlesnake I could imagine that I still heard one. And it was not imagination after all. As I focused the light across the shaft I saw a snake near the same spot I had first seen one, but now only about a foot of its tail was hanging out of a crack in the wall.

To my surprise, I could see the lion. Why she had not gone farther back into the mine I don't know. But there she sat on the old rotten 8x8 timber on the far side of the shaft, spitting and laying back her ears and showing me her teeth as if she planned on staying right where she was.

I was afraid that if I shot the lion where she was she'd fall down the shaft and I would not be able to get her. I picked up some rocks and threw first at the rattlesnake. I hit it a glancing bow, and it crawled farther back in the crack and out of sight. I would have to pass by it if things progressed that far.

Now I could concentrate on the lion. I wanted her off the timber so that she would not fall down the shaft when I shot her. I didn't know yet how I could cross the shaft and get her, for I didn't trust the rotten timber with my weight. But I knew for sure that I would never get her if she fell into the shaft, because when rocks fell into it I could hear them bouncing from side to side and getting fainter and fainter until the sound was only a whisper. It was obviously many hundreds of feet deep.

I knew that if the lion turned and ran back into the tunnel she could get out of sight fast, but I had to take that chance. So I began chucking rocks at her, and my second throw hit her on a front foot and she began backing up. She took her time but kept moving backward along the timber. I could tell that the bright light in her eyes had her confused.

Pretty soon she backed off the timber and onto the solid tunnel floor. I settled down for a shot. I had to hold the light in one and the rifle in the other, and it was pretty awkward.

I leaned against the tunnel wall, and just as I was squeezing off a shot aimed at the lion's head the dogs stopped barking and the snake, or snakes, buzzed. The sound seemed to be right by my ear.

I shot anyway, and the lion turned and ran down the tunnel and out of sight. The shot made a deafening roar that brought down sand and small rocks, and I thought for a moment that the tunnel would cave in. But finally everything except my nerves settled down.

Well, now I had a shut-in lion back there somewhere in the dark and a bottomless hole with rotten timbers and rattlesnakes for a starting place. Things didn't look a bit good. I tested the timber with one foot, and it felt spongy. I didn't dare trust it to hold my weight.

Stamping the timber got me another buzz out of the snake in the right-hand wall. This time the buzzing sounded muffled, as though the snake had crawled farther back in the cracks. Still, I looked hard to make sure a snake wasn't within striking range; but I couldn't see any.

Now I had to either get across the shaft some way or else give the whole thing up. I'm a little ashamed to admit that I considered giving up a few times.

I went outside and began to search for a good strong timber to span the shaft with, but I found something better — a length of old rust two-inch pipe. I tested it and decided that it would hold me up, so I drug it into the mine, placed one end on the old timber, and very slowly and carefully pushed it across the shaft on top of the timber. I could stand on the pipe and reach the right-hand wall to balance myself, so after pounding on the wall and getting only a faint buzz from the snakes, I started across.

When I reached the solid tunnel floor I saw blood and hair. I had hit the lion, but just how badly she was hurt I didn't know.

This tunnel measures about seven feet high by six feet wide — a tight place in which to tangle with a wounded lion. But I had a powerful light that must have shown for 100 feet or more up the tunnel, and besides my rifle I had my .22 Magnum Colt frontier-model handgun on my belt. So I would say I was well armed.

I must have gone about 500 feet into the tunnel when I first spotted something I couldn't make out up ahead. As I got closer I saw that it was a cave-in.

Most of the underground in these mountains is solid rock, but there are a few faults of soft stuff that have to be timbered up. This was such a place. These broken timbers were so old and soft that I could stick my finger right into them. The debris had filled the tunnel about halfway to the ceiling, leaving plenty of room to crawl over. The pile consisted mostly of clay and broken timber mixed with a few rocks.

I saw some plain lion tracks in the soft clay and quite a lot of blood where she had crawled over the muck pile. Of course, I didn't need to see any of this sign to know that she was up ahead somewhere, because up to now there hadn't been any place in the tunnel for her to hide or escape.

I decided that the ceiling looked pretty safe, but I went over the pile fast anyway. On the other side the tunnel forked off in two directions. A plain blood trail led into the the right-hand tunnel. I followed it. I hadn't gone far when I saw something that I thought was the lion. I knew I was spooked, and it was easy to be tricked by the imagination here. What I saw looked like the back end or hip of the lion close up against the left wall. As I watched, I became more convinced that it was.

I figured that she probably was already dead, and I hesitated to shoot so far back in the mine unless it was necessary, because of the terrible concussion that the .30/06 would make

in this underground confinement. I remembered the distur-
bance that my first shot had made only a short way inside the
tunnel. Now I was hundreds of feet underground and was
afraid that a shot would cause more muck to come down at the
cave-in I had crawled over.

But I must have been less afraid of this possibility than I was
of approaching the lion with the uncertainly that she might be
alive and on the fight, because I decided to shoot.

I braced myself against the tunnel wall and was steadying
the rifle and the light for a shot when I saw two green spots
blazing like emeralds in the blackness farther back in the mine.
Of course, I knew at once that this was the lion, and I tried to
level on her with the scope, but the green lights went out. She
had turned her head and was not looking at my light. I stayed
put, and soon she looked again. I put the crosshairs just under
the two green spots and touched off.

Well, I have never heard a canned-up sonic boom, but I can
imagine that the noise and concussion would be similar to
what that old army .30/06 made when it blasted off down there
in the mine. The sound was deafening, and sand and gravel
poured down in a solid cloud. The sounds kept echoing up
and down the many tunnels and shafts in the old mine, gradually becoming weaker and weaker until they faded away
altogether. Then, there was a deathly silence that seemed
almost as bad as the noise.

For what reason I don't know, but I turned off my light. As I
stood there in the silence and total darkness I got a feeling that
a mere description cannot do justice to. The closest I can
come is to say that I felt as if I didn't weigh a pound.

At the crack of the gun I had seen the green eyes and dim
form of the lion flung back, and I felt sure that the bullet had
found its mark. But the lion was just out of the light's reach, so I
was still a bit cautious.

I put the rifle down, took my pistol in one hand and the light
in the other, and slowly advanced. As I drew near I could see
the lion. The impact had flung her back and upended her. She
was very dead. The bullet had entered her cheek and come
out the back of her neck, leaving a large hole.

Well, now I only had to worry about how to get the lion out

and about the cave-in spot between me and the outside world. The first problem was solved when I found that the lion was a rather small female, weighing probably 70 or 80 pounds. There was no doubt: it was Old Smarty. The proper toes were missing, and her teeth were worn and yellow. I don't know whether this was a fitting death for such an interesting and exciting creature, but I can guarantee that she gave me the most dangerous and exciting evening I have ever spent.

I picked her up on my shoulder and was soon at the cave-in much to my relief, nothing had changed there. I felt a little foolish for having thought that perhaps the spot had fallen in from the concussion of my shot. That cave-in has probably looked the same way for 30 or 40 years and may continue on without change for that much longer.

It was a relief to dump Old Smarty over the muck pile and then scrable over myself and get it behind me. When I got back to the entrance and the shaft, I beat on the rattlesnake's side of the tunnel and didn't get a buzz.

I drooped Old Smarty over the old rusty pipe and rotten timber and then sat down astraddle the support with my back to the entrance. Then I scooted myself backward about a foot at a time while keeping the lion balanced and pulling her to me after each scoot. Soon I was across the deep shaft and outside with my barking dogs.

I turned all the dogs loose and let them smell and worry the lion a little, and I am sure Old Squeaker knew that this was Old Smarty who had outsmarted and outrun him so many times over the years. In a way, Old Squeaker was raised up with Old Smarty.

Squeaker ran circles all over the place, jumped on and off me, barked, and made a fool of himself in general, acting just like a six-month-old puppy instead of an eight-year-old dog.

The two young dogs, Eckebod and Blue Boy, looked at Squeaker in a bewildered way, and looked at me as if they were trying to say, "What's the matter, Boss, has our teacher gone nuts?" The End.

OLD YELLER

With all his experiences, Shorty Lyon
can put himself in a bear's shoes!

I had been hearing report of this large yellow bear that had turned cow killer for several years.

My good friend, Blue Rice, on Sacaton Creek twenty miles south of me, had lost a lot of cattle to this bear. Blue is a hunter as well as a rancher, partly out of necessity to protect his stock and partly because he loves to hunt. While just a boy, Blue had hunted with the famous Ben Lilly. He keeps a pack of good hound dogs, and lives in some of the best bear and lion country left in these United States, so he does a lot of hunting.

When I told Blue that this big yellow bear had moved in on my little ranch at Mogollon, Blue said, "Shorty, if that is the bear I think it is, you are in for a lot of trouble, because everytime he comes to my ranch, he kills some cattle." When I ask why he had not caught him, he replied that that was much easier said than done. He said, "I have tried everything and never had any luck getting him. He is as trap wise as a coyote, and he has whipped my dogs until I have only one left that will trail him. If you can get that Old Yeller son-of-a-gun, my hat is off to you."

Besides what Blue had said about this bear, Joe Hooker, also an old timer, living on a ranch on Bear Creek thirty-five miles south of here, told me that at one time he had borrowed all the dogs in the country, and had as many as twenty-five dogs after Old Yeller. "I got several dogs killed, but still failed to stop him," he said. He also added that he was too smart to eat poison and was trap wise. Joe said, "If you start trapping for him, he usually leaves out for a spell then comes back." Joe was hoping that I would get him.

Arthur Balke, ten miles to the north, and many more ranchers on the west slope of the Mogollons, had suffered from Old Yeller's raids, and were wishing me luck too.

So in realizing that this was a bear of unusual intelligence, and knowing a great deal about bears, it was easy to conjure up the reason for this particular bear becoming so smart.

Old Yeller was no ordinary bear. He may have been a nice little roll-a-polly cub at some time in the past, and perhaps spent his first summer high up in the mountains eating berries, ants, and grubs, sucking warm, rich milk from his mother, and playing with his sister. But that was a long time ago.

When I first knew him, he had lived a long time and learned a lot. He had long since lost his cute little baby cub ways and he had also lost his appetite for grubs and berries. They no longer filled his great stomach fast enough to satisfy his hunger. It now required a hundred pounds or more of good red meat. This much meat would put him in a satisfied mood for a day's sleep, but upon awakening and relieving himself in the dusk of evening, he was ready for another meal of the same portion.

His first memory of the change from ordinary bear diet to the eating of cattle, no doubt, came early in his life. It was probably an unusual dry spring in the Mogollon Mountains when his mother, a large black bear, and his smaller sister, also a black, were hard put to find enough to eat. The wise old mother had quit the higher mountains and brought her two yearling cubs down to the foot hills.

This was ranch country, and in good years the bears left it strickly alone for men lived and ruled here. Man with his gun, traps, dogs, and poison was to be feared very much. Other than man, the bears had no enemies that they feared. But when they were forced to invade man's domain, they knew that they had to be smart and careful if they expected to ever return to their home in the high mountains. One mistake and this super animal man would kill them with one of his many devices that he so cunningly concealed and managed.

On this first venture into the cattle country, Yeller learned a lot. One of his very first lessons was not to go dashing head long into a good smelling dead cow, no matter how good the stench of the decaying meat and the maggots were. He had to approach with the utmost caution. This he learned in no uncertain terms from a tremendous whack from Mamma bear, that sent him rolling, made his ears ring, and half stunned him. There were no doubts or half way measures about it; when Mamma said, "No," in this manner, he got the message.

He then waited and watched to see how it should be done. He saw his mother test the air in all directions, then smell the ground with the utmost care as she circled the dead cow, and when she had got very close she became even more careful and concentrated on one particular spot smelling and scratching at it with the utmost caution. As far as Yeller could tell, it seemed to be a lot of unnecessary delay. He could see nothing to be afraid of, and he was hungry and anxious to get at this good smelling food. The saliva ran from each side of his mouth until it touched the ground where he sat.

But just when it seemed that he could not bear to wait any longer, the earth suddenly burst up from where his mother was scratching. Bits of gravel and sticks flew into the air. There was a loud angry snap and a large rusty object lay exposed where seconds before there had not been anything at all.

All three bears dashed back into the bushes. Yeller had seen his first bear trap, and smart little bear that he was he immediately realized that here was something to be respected and feared.

In fact, he was now afraid to approach the dead cow where a short time ago he had wanted to rush in. But after his mother had ventured back and settled down to eating, his sister first joined her, and the sound of eating and the smell was more than he could stand so he also joined in the feast, but this time with the utmost caution.

And what a feast it was. Here was a thousand pounds of rich food that could be gulped down in great mouth fulls. It was no wonder that after such a meal he would not be satisfied to dig and turn over large rocks and logs only to get a small bug or perhaps an even smaller grub.

Now this particular cow happened to be a large fat one that had died from black leg and laid in the warm sun for three days, so it was easy to come by.

The rancher had seen bear tracks in the area and knowing it was a natural bait had set the trap hoping to catch the bears before they did kill some of his cattle, as he felt sure they would after they had cleaned up this dead one.

Yes, Yeller had learned a lot here at his first feast on cow meat, but this was only the beginning. Before the summer was over, he was to witness the terrible experience of his smaller sister's death, who had eaten a piece of meat near a cow that the mother bear had killed two days before. His sister had rushed in ahead of him upon returning to the kill and gulped down the meat even though the mother was growling a protest at her disregard for caution.

The poison was deadly and quick. His small sister turned to the mother for help, but fell to the ground after only a few steps. Froth and blood formed on her mouth. Her eyes were glazed, and her pitiful cries and groans, as she rolled on the ground, were something Yeller would always remember even though they only lasted a short while. She was soon dead on her back with her feet pointing up into the air in a most unnatural position. And although his mother did make some unmistakable whimpering sounds of motherly love, she nevertheless left the area immediately with Yeller close on her heels.

Before this summer had passed, Yeller also learned what it was to be chased by large packs of big vicious dogs. Dogs that could smell even better than he and his mother, and could follow their trail no matter how hard they tried to lose them.

On one occasion, he had run until he was out of breath. His lungs burned like fire, and his feet were torn and bleeding. He could go no further, and had fallen exhausted to the ground where the dogs found him and fell upon him with the intent of tearing him into pieces. He had put up what resistence he could in his exhausted condition, but even if he had not have been completely given out, he would have been no match for this howling, tearing pack.

There would come a day when he had only contempt for

man's dogs, but that time had not yet arrived. He was only a little more than a year old now and no bigger than some of the hounds, and there were many of them. In fact, so many that they seemed to be everywhere, and although he was brave and fought the best he could, they soon had him down and would have no doubt killed him in a short time. But this short time they were not allowed.

There was a terrible roar, a popping of teeth, a thudding of blows, and dogs were knocked through the air and scattered like chaf in a whirl wind. And indeed a whirl wind it was as his mother with her tremendous strength, her mother's love, and her terrible anger fell upon the pack with tooth and claw.

Some, who were unfortunate enough to be hit with a solid blow, were dead before they hit the ground. Others, who were able, ran for their life, but there were still others who were braver that stood their ground. One of these, growing over bold, rushed in as his companions were nipping at the she bear's rump, but this was a sad mistake. She grabbed him by the breast and shook him as though he had been a rat. Then placing a foot on him, she enveloped his whole head in her mouth and clamped down. There was a crunching sound and blood and brains spilled out on either side of her great jaws. She then dropped the limp, lifeless form, and charged into the few remaining dogs, all of whom fled before her angry charge.

Yeller got to his feet and started licking his wounds. He had recovered his wind, but his feet still bled and he now bled in a dozen other places where the hounds had bit and ripped him.

He wanted to stay there and rest, but his mother insisted that they move on. He knew by now that she was always right, and he could tell that there was even greater danger down below by the way she tested the wind and her nervous actions. He too tested the wind, and there came to his senitive nose the pungent sweet man smell mixed with the sweat of horses. The smell was strong and close at hand, so he turned and ran, his sore feet entirely forgotten.

But even as he ran there was a tremendous roar, a new sharp flash of pain in his rump, and a new smell, the smell of gun powder. He saw his mother turn down hill ahead of him, and he followed her. She soon had him out of range of the rancher's gun. He was not mortally wounded, and the few dogs that were able to follow them did not have the courage or stamina to do them any real harm.

This time, thanks to his wise old mother, he had escaped with his life, but what of the next time and the next. His mother might not be there. So even though Yeller was yet only a small yearling cub, the lesson of survival was indelibled on his mind with a lasting impression.

Summer changed into fall, and with the autumn, there were acorns, pinon, and other nuts to feed on. Yeller and his mother forged on these with an occasional feast of meat, because the she bear, out of necessity, had long since become a killer.

So when time for the long sleep arrived, the two were fat and ready for their hibernation. Mamma bear was now extremely careful, and at times when she would hear hounds that were miles and miles away, she would immediately move on to a safer place as she realized that the extra fat she had stored for the winter's hibernation would make it impossible to outrun the dogs for any distance.

At last the weather changed and winter came in earnest. There was some permanent ice and snow now. Mother and son climbed high upon the northside of the old Mogollon Baldy Mountain. Here they found a small over hanging cliff where they cleaned a hole just big enough to curl up in. Then eating a few dry spruce and pine needles, they moved in and lay down for a long sleep, which would last probably four months or more depending on the weather.

This was to be Yeller's last sleep with his mother. Come spring, he would have to start taking care of himself since Mamma would then be looking for a papa bear, another love making period and a brand new family that would be born while she was in hiberation the next winter.

And so it happened that when the two came forth in the spring, Mamma was extremely cross with little Yeller, who was two years old now and not so little. Finally they did meet up with a very large papa bear, and he was even more cross than Mamma with poor Yeller. So with the two of them continually abusing him, he gave up in despair and struck off to make a life of his own.

The two years with his wise old mother had been well spent. She had taught him well, and he had been a very intelligent pupil, quick to catch on to anything of importance to his survial. Fate too was kind to Yeller, so with the combination of luck and intelligence, he lived to a ripe old age.

He ranged over a vast amount of country. Beside the Mogollon Mountains that were his home, he had explored the Black Range to the east and had ventured, a few times, as far west as the White Mountains in Arizona. In all these wonderings, he had been careful never forgetting his early training and also the many many things he had learned during his long and dangerous life of perhaps 30 years or more. He could truly be called a smart old bear, and was probably the very wisest of all the bears that roamed the great Gila Forest of Southwest New Mexico.

In fact, it had begun to look like Old Yeller would finally die of old age. Probably during one of his long sleeps, he would pass on into the really long sleep the sleep from which no one or no thing has ever come back to tell about. In a way, it is a pity that this did not happen to him. It would have been a very fitting demise for such a magnificent creature as he surely was.

But such was not the case, and since fate had indeed been kind to him for many years, he had lived an extremely long healthful life for a bear. He had killed an untold number of cattle, sheep, hogs, goats, and even a few horses. He had alluded hundreds of chases, had stopped and killed dogs by the dozens, and then fled before men could get in range of him with their rifles. He could detect any poison at the first smell. He also knew about traps, and delighted in springing them, up-setting them, and sometime leaving a huge pile of droppings on top of them. He could stand a quarter of a mile from a ranch house and know whether or not the rancher was away or at home. If he was not at home, he would come to the house, tear down the door and help himself to whatever he found there. The clamor of the dogs in their pens bothered him not in the least. If a dog was not in the pen, or tied, and was foolish enough to make trouble for him, he soon killed it or run it off. If the rancher was at home, he knew it, and he never showed himself. The one thing he respected and feared was the rancher with this rifle.

Now all these years. Old Yeller had been doing his marauding on ranches and had been matching wits with these ranchers, and it is to be admitted that these ranchers are capable and smart. It is a wonder that he had been able to outsmart them for so long, and would have probably continued on doing so had he not found a different kind of a rancher.

Of course, Old Yeller had no way of knowing that this ranch belonged to Shorty Lyon, and that Shorty was not only a rancher, but that he was also a professional predator hunter and trapper, and where the ordinary rancher had quite a lot of experience in protecting his stock from predators, which included bears, they had worked at the job of tracking down or trapping these animals only as a part time job when their livestock was threatened, whereas Shorty Lyon had put in his full time for 50 years as a predatory hunter and trapper. He had spent the better part of a life time studying the habits of wild animals and was as skilled and cunning at the art of capturing them as Old Yeller was skilled in his art of avoiding man's efforts and devices to capture him.

So when Old Yeller did move in on Shorty Lyon's little ranch at Mogollon, New Mexico, it immediately became a contest of wits between two old timers, one of them a great bear of the Mogollon's and the other a famous trapper and hunter. The contest was not as one sided as some might think.

Shorty and his wife arrived home from one of his hunting camps one morning to find the back door torn off the house. Old Yeller had made a call, ate one hundred pounds of dog food, scattered things about, left a huge pile of droppings on top of everything and left. He had not been gone long. Shorty's dogs could smell the scent and were clammering to be turned loose after him. They did not have more than two or three minutes to wait. Shorty got his gun, turned his four dogs loose and took off.

Not far from the ranch house was Cooney Canyon, a large canyon of bluffs hundreds of feet high with crevices, over hanging bluffs, and rock slides, an idea place for a bear to make a get away. Old Yeller lost no time in going off into this upside down country. Whenever the dogs caught up to him, he whipped them back, and he stayed under the over hanging bluffs or in the thick brush never letting Shorty catch sight of him. It soon became too hot for the dogs, and all returned to the ranch.

This was just the first day and the beginning of a six day battle between Shorty Lyon, his dogs, traps, gun, and Old Yeller.

During these six days, Shorty ran old Yeller four times with his dogs. Each time he whipped the dogs back, slid off in Cooney Canyon, and stayed out of sight of Shorty with his scope sighted rifle.

Old Yeller also killed three calves belonging to Shorty during these six days. Shorty set traps at these kills, pegging the remains of the calves down, and taking the utmost care in setting the traps. In these trap sets, Shorty used all the skills he had learned in years of trapping experiences, placing, covering, and camouflaging the traps with the utmost care. When he had finished making the sets, the place looked as if nothing had been disturbed. But none of this fooled the wise Old Yeller bear.

The few times that he returned to the kills where the traps were, he either stepped over or around the traps or gently pulled them out of the ground. Some of them he threw, some he just left setting on top of the ground in plain sight while he ate what he wanted of the calf's remains.

Shorty's wife, Louise, began to get desperate after the third calf was killed. She wanted to call in outside help, but Shorty would not agree to this. His reputation as a trapper and hunter of long standing was at a stake. He said, "I will lose a lot of cattle before I'll admit that this damn yeller bear is smarter than I am." "But," he added, "It shore looked like he might be at that."

Now Shorty had set a huge grizzly bear trap at his back door the very next night after the bear had torn the door down. He had carried old rotten hay, that his hogs had bedded down in, from the barn, and placed this big trap well down under the hay. During the day, he placed some strong boards over the trap, and took them off by night. The bear had not come near the house again, but had stopped a short distance away, except one night, he did come near the dog pen, and relieved himself of a great pile of calf hair and bones, while the dogs barked and charged at him, but could not break out of their pen. And Shorty, hearing all this, waited, expecting Old Yeller to step in the trap at the back door at any moment, but he never did.

So on the sixth night, Shorty and his wife, Louise, decided to spend the night with their son and his family at Alma, 8 miles down in the San Francisco River Valley below Mogollon.

They did this, and of course, Old Yeller knew they were gone. By this time, he was, no doubt, hungry for a little dessert to go with the meat diet, so he decided to make another raid on the ranch house.

The dogs barking in their pen close by disturbed him not. He approached the same door that he had torn off the hinges six days before. It had been repaired, but this did not concern him. He would easily tear it up again. He smelled the ground and the only scent that he got was old musty hay and hog smell. This was not to be feared, so he took a step forward, his foot sinking a little as it often did in soft dirt. There was a sudden explosion. The huge trap had him high up his leg. He ran backward, snarling and bitting, dragging the trap with its extra length of chain and hook.

The dogs in the near by pen went frantic. They knew now that Old Yeller was in trouble.

In the first few seconds of surprise and pain, Old Yeller ran in a confused rampage tearing up and destroying everything in his path. Then reason returned, and he headed away from the ranch house for the high bluffs. Several times the hook on the trap chain caught on small trees, and he tore them down or broke them up with his huge old teeth and claws. But at last the hook caught in a grove of trees that he could not tear loose from. Still he did not give up. Old Warrier that he was, he fought the terrible trap with all of his might, and was slowly but surely cutting off his leg. If given time, he would still survive.

But this time was not allowed. When Shorty and Louise returned early in the morning, there was the big hole at the back door, the sign of the trap and drag going off the mountain, and the dogs still frantically barking.

Shorty let the dogs out. They made a bee-line off the moun-

109

tain for the bear. Gun in hand, Shorty followed as fast as he could, with Lousie coming behind.

It was no time until the dogs were fighting him. He hit at them with his one free front foot, the other being in the trap, and when he hit, his blows jarred the ground. If he had of connected, there would have been dead dogs. But the dogs knew that they had the advantage of him, and they bored in and bit him on the rump and sides staying out of the way of his sledge hammer blows.

As soon as Shorty got up close, he leveled his rifle, and shot Old Yeller through the heart. He was in a hurry to do this, partly to be sure that he did not kill one of his dogs, but mostly to get the old bear out of his pain.

After all Shorty and Old Yeller had a lot in common. They were both wise old timers, and whether or not Old Yeller knew, this one cannot say, but it was a weird thing that happened. Upon being shot, the old bear realized that his time was up at last, and he pointed his nose to the sky and gave forth his death cry in a long plaintive and mournful sound. Shorty recognized it as such, felt sorry for him, even though he had killed his cattle, tore up his home, and insulted him in the worst possible manner.

The fact still remained, that it was a privilege to share this earth with one as great as Old Yeller. The End.

BEARS

. . . Controversy & Conservation

The true story of the idea for "Old Yeller".

It was a mighty dry spring and summer here at Mogollon this year.

I had backed my truck down to the water of an almost dry tank, and was arranging some timbers so that I could dip up water and fill the barrels when my 11 year old grandson, Tol Feather, exclaimed, "Grandpa, look here at these big tracks in the mud!"

When I saw the extra large bear track, I automatically thought of the cow with the big bag that I had seen a few days back. There was no absolute evidence that a bear had killed her calf, but seeing these tracks sure made me think that one might have.

To say that all bears are killers or to say that bears don't kill cattle is as ridiculous as it would be to say that all men are killers or that no man will kill.

But we certainly do have plenty of people who are extremists when the talk turns to bears. There are some folks, mainly ranchers, who have suffered losses from bears, that think the only kind of good bear is a dead one. While on the other hand there are some others who are just as sure that a bear never kills anything and eats only grubs, roots, berries, and nuts. These are usually city folks that have never owned any livestock in bear country.

Well, I certainly don't think a bear should be killed just because he turned over a garbage can, but I do believe that he should be killed if he is killing livestock.

I was not sure yet just which kind of a bear had moved in with me, but seeing his tracks there with the cattle tracks sure made me nervous.

I saddled my mule and took a ride looking for the cow with the big bag and for a possible kill. Well, I found both. The cow's bag was now spoiled and she was bawling near the remains of her calf. There wasn't much left of the calf but enough to identify it as a bear kill even if there had not been bear droppings all around.

Bears have a peculiar way of rolling the hide of their victims, which is unmistable once you have seen it.

When I arrived back at the house it was too late to call the Game and Fish Department's office at Las Cruces but I drove to Alma and spent the night with my son. Early the next morning, I drove to Glenwood and called the Game and Fish Department and reported what I had found, and asked for a permit to take the bear. Mr. Marion Embrey, Area Supervisor, said to go ahead and get the bear and that a permit would follow immediately.

The Depatment of Game and Fish have a very lenient policy so that no time will be lost for taking a killer bear once the evidence is found that it is a killer. I will quote in part from a Depredation Permit issued by the Department.

"Upon receipt of report of depredation, the Director of the Game and Fish Department shall charge a member of the Game Department with the responsibility of investigating the depredation report at the earliest possible moment. (Please note this next paragraph):

"In the meanwhile, if depredation is by a bear, the landowner or lesser may take such action as may be necessary to protect his property until receipt of permit."

Well so much for bears in general, and back to my own private bear.

When I reached home I was in for a surprise. This bear was not waiting for me to attack. He had carried the attack to me and in a big way. He had torn the back door off my house, went in and had eaten about 100 pounds of expensive dog food, tore up, scattered, and wrecked everything else in the room where he had entered. Then he had gone by the dog pen and to show his contempt for my four big hounds and four little pups, which had no doubt been raising plenty of ruckus while he had been eating the feed and wrecking the house, he stopped near the dog pen and relieved himself. This was really adding insult to injury.

I got my gun and turned the dogs out as quick as I could. They took off in a wild clamor. It looked like we would soon have us a bear. The dogs were running, I was running, and the wife and Tol were running, but the country was steep and I soon gave out. Before I did, I heard the dogs fighting and supposed they had already overtaken Mr. Bear. However, I soon knew I was mistaken when I heard the yapping of coyotes mixing in the fight.

What had happened might seem fantastic to some people but not to a predator hunter. Very often coyotes will throw in with a killer bear or lion and follow him around to clean up his kills and sometimes make kills of their own if necessary. I don't imagine that the bears or lions appreciate these henchmen, but they have to put up with them anyway. This bunch of coyotes didn't seem to want my dogs to bother their good provider, so they scattered them and decoyed them off the bear's trail.

Well, that was just one of the many mishaps that followed for the next five days. I sure had myself a problem. This particular bear was really a smart old-timer. I soon learned that he was trap wise and was not afraid of the dogs.

He killed another calf that night in less than a quarter of a mile of the house, then came down near the dog pen and repeated his insulting performance of relieving himself of a great pile of calf hair, bones, and dog feed.

We took after him again the next morning and trailed him about one mile to Mineral Creek north of our house. There are 400-foot bluffs, caves, and whip back the dogs and go off in a crevice and in under the over-hanging bluffs. I tried in vain to get in sight of him.

It would have taken a dozen or more of the most ferocious dogs to have stopped this bear much less tree him. He was also as trap wise as any coyote and this is very unusual for a bear.

But persistence finally did paid off. After several fruitless chases and attempts at trapping, he did get too anxious for another treat of expensive dog food, and I caught him in a large bear trap at the back door he had torn down several days earlier.

He left running down the mountain with this big trap, and the drag looked like a turning plow had been drug. He pulled up some small trees, ate up some, but finally hung up on one too strong to tear up about one-half mile from the house.

I turned the dogs out and they made a bee-line for him. They knew they had the advantage at last. When I got there, the fight was really hot and I was afraid for my dogs. He was hitting at them with sledge hammer blows that shook the ground. If he had connected there would have been a dead dog for sure.

I shot the old fellow and he gave forth one of the most pitiful cries I have ever heard. He knew he was through, and even though he had torn up my house, killed my cattle, and insulted and embarrassed me in the most humiliating manner, when he gave this death cry I felt real sorry for him. If you asked me, bears are too damn human anyway! The End.

PREDATOR CONTROL PAYS HIGH DIVIDENDS ON DIAMOND BAR RANCH

Editor's Note: In the spring of 1962 the owners of the Diamond Bar Ranch decided to do something about the coyotes that were taking a heavy toll on their calf crop, so they contacted Alton Ford. Alton couldn't go at the time, but he passed the information on to T.J. "Shorty" Lyon, Game and Fish Department trapper.

Mr. Lyon has been a trapper, hunter, and rancher all his life. He moved to New Mexico in 1931 from Oklahoma, and homesteaded near Quemado, and says, "in those lean days, if it had not been for coyote skins and pinon nuts, I would have never made it." In 1936, he and his family moved to Mogollon, where he operates a small cattle ranch. He has worked for the U.S. Forest Service; U.S. Fish and Wildlife Service, and for the past 18 years has been with the New Mexico Department of Game and Fish as a lion hunter and coyote trapper.

In past years some of his lion hunting experiences have been published in Outdoor Life Magazine.

Following is the account he wrote following his trapping assignment in the summer of 1962:

When C.E. Davis and W.W. Hill bought the Diamond Bar Ranch last winter, they didn't waste any time starting in to improve and develop it into a more efficient and profitable spread.

The Diamond Bar was a ranch anyone would be proud of

Trapping is an Art . . . "a drop of bait for a well-set trap" (even a four-legged animal prefers a smooth place to step, and will be very interested in a whiff of this special concoction).

when they bought it. It's in real picturesque country in the Black Range Mountains in Southwestern New Mexico, and runs 1200 head of mother cows that range from the top of the Black Range Mountains to the Gila River. This is some of the best cow country that can be found, but these new owners knew how to make it into just a little better home for a white faced cow so they set in to do a lot of smart things.

In my opinion one of the first and smartest of these was to keep old Bob Thorn on the payroll. Bob had been there long enough to have a lot of savvy about the ranch, the stock, and anything else that might contribute to the welfare of a cow. So when Bob told these new owners and their foreman, Mr. Jack Birchard, that he figgered the Diamond Bar had been losing around 100 head of calves to the coyotes every year, they listened to what he had to say, and beside listening to what he had to say they did something about it. They set in to find and hire a trapper, something that is not too easy to do nowadays.

Twenty-five years ago there were plenty of good trappers, but times have changed. The price of furs dropped until trapping has not been profitable, and the Department of Game and Fish changed their polices from predatory control to biological and technical studies. These two factors alone made trapping unprofitable and therefore uninteresting, so than young men no longer learned the art. (And it certainly is an art.) Old trappers went to work at other jobs and died.

But El Coyote didn't go to work at any different job nor did he die off. No, far from it. He multiplied and stayed with his same old job which was mainly eating. First he cleaned out the rabbits here in the Black Range, the deer were next, and when they became scarce he turned to calves.

What Mr. Birchard wanted was a full time trapper, and in trying to locate one he had contacted my friend, Alton Ford, at Silver City. Now Alton is one of the best trappers in the state, but he had children in school and a good job so he passed the information on to me.

I am one of the few Game and Fish trappers in the state and had a job, but I had 30 days annual leave coming. So when Mr. Birchard got in touch with me we made a deal for me to trap a month on the Diamond Bar.

Well when I arrived and started to work there were little bob tail calves all over the place, and if you stopped to listen on almost any high ridge you would hear some old cow with a full bag bawling for her calf. Believe me, this is no joke to a rancher with beef at 30 cents on the hoof and all the responsibility and expense of a big ranch.

I never worked for a better outfit. Everyone pitched in and helped anyway they could. I stayed at the Lynx place on Main Diamond Creek, and there were four cowboys there, Bob, Bud, Jerry and Roy. They all helped me run my traps when they could do so and take care of their own job. They killed what coyotes they found in my traps and reported any new kills or coyotes they saw and cows that had recently lost their calves. All this was a great help and was very much appreciated.

I worked hard too and put 112 traps out on approximately 120 miles of ranch road. My wife accompanied me and cooked our noon day meal of beef steak furnished by the ranch, and she also helped me trail down any coyotes that happened to pull up a trap stake or break the trap chain loose.

When we would get in from a long day's work usually after dark, Mrs. "Babe" Thorn, Bob's wife, would be there waiting for us with something good to eat and some cheerful, friendly words that always made the day's work seem easier.

Space will not permit me to tell of the many individual adventures we encountered with old smart coyotes that were hard to trap and many other interesting happenings in that unforgettable month on the Diamond Bar Ranch, but I will close by giving the facts and figures of our stay there.

We caught and killed 56 coyotes; 24 of these were females. We were there during the whelping season and we counted 113 wet tits and unborn pups. I feel confident that we saved more than 100 calves. This will mean approximately $10,000 this fall. I was paid $340.00 and expenses which all totaled probably ran close to $500.00 which would equal 2000% on the investment.

I don't understand some ranchers that are willing to pay for so many other expenses but still will not spend a dime for predatory control. In my opinion, a calf saved from a coyote, eagle, lion, or bear is worth just as much to a rancher as one saved from any other cause.

What we need is more predator control. This old song that is being sung about the balance of nature and the rabbit controlling coyote is OK if El Coyote is living off someone else's stock, but if he moved in on theirs the singers change their tune in a hurry. I've seen it happen many times. The End.

Cleaning a trap before it is reset.

The Pick-up Cowboy
by Shortfellow

I know a bunch of cowboys
That's what they claim to be,
But the way they haul their horses around
Is something you should see.

I always thought real cowboys
Sat on a horse's back,
But all of them that pass my house
Have pick-ups with a rack.

The horses in these pick-up racks
Look very fine and fat.
They toss their heads, and paw the floor
They're mightly good for that.

I think perhaps that they could walk
If the occasion did demand,
But really there's no use of it
With this pick-up cowboy man.

Sometimes they go at break neck speed,
Sometimes they travel slow,
But regardless of the pace they set,
They do make quite a show.

The horses know to brace themselves
For quick stops and sudden turns.
The cowboys also are aware
Of the pick-ups unconcern.

They both can ride, I'm telling you,
All kinds of roads they've tried.
This pick-up cowboy and his horse
And the pick-up is their pride.